Rock Me

Victoria
McFarlane

Previously Published as Rock Me by V McFarlane

NOTE FROM AUTHOR

ROCK ME is written in British English and contains British spelling and grammar.

This may appear incorrect to some readers when compared to US English books.

Stay Fierce xo

One

Ray

I push through the thick crowd of the sports bar, shoving my way through the group of suits and shouldering past the college kids. It was the only way to get anywhere in this bar and mostly, people ignored it, stumbling once before resuming their conversations.

If you came to Franks, you expected it with how popular the place is.

My attire, however, isn't something I'd wear here. No, this was a jeans and tee kind of joint, not tight, curve fitting dresses and heels type. I stood out like a sore thumb, even the suits had casual-ed up their work wear, ditching the jackets and rolling up their sleeves, popping the buttons at the collar. There was nothing I could do with this dress.

"Ray!" Harper yells from the booth near the bar. By

the looks of it, she's on her third cosmo and by the flush in her cheeks she's already halfway to drunk.

I slide into the booth and finally take a breath.

To say I'd had a shitty evening would be an understatement. I must give out a vibe that entices creeps. With the string of bad dates I've had lately it's got to be something I'm doing.

"Do I have 'assholes welcome' written on my forehead?" I ask Harper, hanging my head.

"Oh sweetie," Harper pouts, "That bad huh?"

"Bad doesn't seem to cut it, do you wanna know what he asked me?" I stare at her dead in the eye, daring her to guess.

"What?" She places the straw between her pink lips and sucks.

"He asked me if my boobs were real." I scoff.

Harper's brows shoot up, "Oh, what did you say?"

"I told him that it was none of his business but yes they are real and then he told me to prove it!" I cringe, remembering the way his beady eyes roamed over me, undressing me piece by piece.

"I was so shocked by that, that he took it as an invitation!" I shudder, "Safe to say I got the fuck out of there."

Harper's mouth is hanging open, her green eyes wide, "That did not happen!"

"It did!" Olivia, our friend, and waitress here at Franks slides an old fashioned in front of me. "I love you!" I tell her, picking up the drink and taking a healthy sip. I groan as it hits my taste buds and finally let my shoulders relax.

"Harper warned me that you'd had *another* shitty date."

"I'm just giving up on men," I declare, "I'm joining our Harper here and going celibate."

"Hey!" Harper shrills, "Celibacy is not my first choice I just," she waves a hand in front of her face, "Have no idea how to deal with men. Or social situations."

I laugh, "That's true."

Harper shrugs and I turn back to Olivia, "Seriously, I don't even want to tell you how horrible it was."

Olivia eyes me sympathetically, "I'm off in an hour, I'll join you then and you can tell me all about it. Where's Vivian tonight?"

I think about our final friend that makes up our little group and my boss and shrug, "Her schedule tells me she's at some function tonight with the guys at *Dress*."

"That fashion magazine?"

I nod, "I'll text her though."

Oli nods and disappears into the crowd of the bar, collecting glasses on her way. A few guys whistle at her and make attempts to grab her attention but she simply flips them off and continues on her way. Hell, if I could just be more like her maybe I wouldn't have these issues. That woman is fierce as hell and doesn't take any shit from any man. She's beautiful too.

Our Harper is the quiet one of the group, the one who hides behind a book rather than make actual conversation, Vivian is the socialite, the successful model and woman all men get on their knees for and me? Hell, I have no idea what I am.

I sigh into my glass, allowing a few seconds to feel sorry for myself.

Tonight was just one in the many bad dates I've had recently. I've been grabbed inappropriately, spoken to like a piece of meat rather than an actual human being and propositioned more times than I care to admit.

3

I pull out my phone and delete the dating app. Clearly that's part of the issue seeing as all the men I've seen lately have been from there.

"Giving up?" Harper asks, watching me.

"I'm taking a break. A man hiatus. There's nothing wrong with being single."

"That's right," Harper nods once, slurping up the last of her cocktail. "Want another?" She nods to my already half-finished old fashioned. I nod and watch her as she slides her way to the bar, head low, almost sinking into herself to make herself as small as possible. I've known Harper my entire life, we grew up together and she's always been this way. She gets louder after a few drinks but throw her into a crowd and she'll do everything possible to just disappear.

I fidget in my seat. God, I wish I got changed before I came here but I just yelled the address at the cab driver after I ran out of the restaurant and away from the creep. He followed me out and made a move to grab me before I threw myself into the back of the car but thankfully, I was quicker. I may have been in heels but never underestimate a woman on a mission to get the fuck away from someone, especially some dirtbag who thought it appropriate to ask about my breasts on the first date – I say *date* lightly, I was there less than an hour.

The date started out normal and I actually thought, *yes! Finally!* Until about halfway through the appetizers his eyes started to wander down to the cleavage of my dress. It's not even that low of a cut, just shows off the tops of my breasts but I am rather large in that department considering the size of me so they always look bigger and more in your face despite what I wear. After a few minutes he still hadn't looked back at my face, so I called him out.

He didn't even blush about being caught.

With a shrug of his shoulders he leaned back and hooked an arm around the back of his chair. "They real?" He smirked.

I had no idea what to say. I was completely shocked at how direct he was and probably resembled some sort of fish out of water with the way my mouth opened and closed as I searched for a response. I honestly thought after telling him they were real he would leave it but oh no, apparently that just spurred him on and after he asked me to prove it and I didn't tell him no, he leaned across the table, fully prepared to grope me there and then in the middle of the restaurant.

He didn't get close. I threw myself back so quickly the chair tipped over and the table rattled, the water in my glass splashing over the rim.

"Don't touch me!" I shrieked. Before he could get another word in, I was beelining for the door, ignoring the stares of the other patrons and the not so hushed whispers and was thanking the stars there was cab parked outside when I finally broke through the doors.

"Raynie, wait!" He had yelled from somewhere close behind me. I felt his fingers brush the top of my arm as I jumped into the cab and I wouldn't be surprised if the door hit him as I slammed it closed.

Good. It would have the least he deserved.

The cabbie kept eyeing me in the rear-view mirror as he drove his way over here. It wasn't a leer, more of a sympathetic look. He was my dads age, greying at the temples with laughter lines at the edges of his eyes.

I tipped him well when I got out.

And now I'm here, sat in the pretty dress I wore for my date, sulking because all the men I've met have been complete pigs.

Maybe I just have too higher of expectations. I blame all the romance books Harper keeps feeding me. She owns a small bookstore in the city, one that doubles up as a coffee shop and when I finish one, she's already picked out another.

No. I'm allowed to have high expectations. What's the point in settling for someone who won't make you happy? And I certainly don't deserve to be treated the way some of these men have treated me.

I sink into my chair and drain my glass of alcohol, scanning the heavy crowd. Hardly surprising on a Friday night and there was a game tonight. The crowd is young, ranging from college aged to maybe mid thirties with a few older guys and girls dotted around.

Me and girls have been coming here for years. It's where Harper and I first met Oli and I introduced the girls to Vivian. We're now an inseparable group of four. I fire off a text to Vivian letting her know we're here for drinks just as Harper is sliding back into the booth. I take a sip of my fresh drink and continue my scan of the bar.

There's a high table just to the left of us, close to the door where two men sit. I recognise one of them as a regular here but the other I don't. He's decorated in dark ink, it swirls around his arms, etched into his olive skin and even from here I can see that he's handsome.

"Oh, you spotted him," Harper giggles, "I noticed him earlier."

"Who is he?" I ask.

Harper shrugs, "I don't know, been in here since I got here."

My eyes flick back to him and suddenly he's looking at me. His eyes boring right into mine. I look away quickly.

I know bad news when I see it and he's got it written all over him.

I throw myself into a conversation with Harper, forcing myself to focus on her and not the guy on the other side of the bar. Truthfully, I want to study his features, follow the lines of his face until I've committed it memory. The man was beautiful to look at, a work of art but I refuse to give in.

After the string of bad experiences I've had, I won't do it again anytime soon. If I were to date, someone safe would be best, a banker or, I don't know, a doctor maybe? Someone serious.

My phone pings with a message from Vivian, telling me she'll be here within the hour and whilst we wait, I spin the glass in front of me, my fingers wet with condensation.

I can't help but feel eyes boring into the back of my head. It sends tingles down my spine and causes my hair to stand on end. I allow myself a peek but when I turn it isn't the tatted guy staring at me, in fact, I can't see anyone looking directly at me.

With a frown I direct my attention at the story Harper's telling me about a new book she's reading and before long the other girls join us and I start to ease, my shoulder's relaxing, my breathing becoming slower.

It's got more to do with the alcohol rather than the atmosphere, but I'll take it.

Vivian flicks a strand of brunette hair off her shoulder and grins, showing off her perfectly white teeth, "Guess who I met tonight!?"

She doesn't wait for an answer, instead, throws back her shot of fireball whiskey and wiggles her shoulders.

"Nate Sandford," she reveals, "And holy shit guys, he's hotter in person! I didn't even think that was possible!"

Harper blushes and I cock my head at her, "Do you have a crush on him?"

"Oh please," she giggles nervously, "Everyone has a crush on Nate Sandford."

"That's true," Oli agrees, tipping her beer to her lips, "Did you get his number?"

"No," Vivi pouts, "But his agent asked me to get in contact for a possible feature in his next music video."

I laugh, "I guess I should make a note to ask Hudson to reach out?"

Her eyes go wide, "Yes! Do that!"

I roll my eyes but schedule it for Monday. As her assistant I do most things for her, emails, scheduling, getting her coffee. It's not as bad as you might think, sure, if she were difficult it would be, but Vivi is nothing like some of the celebrities I've worked with. It's why we've become such great friends. She hated the idea of having an assistant when I was first hired and wouldn't let me do anything for her, not until she started going to all those interviews and photoshoots and parties and she realised she needed me.

As the girls talk about Nate's latest single, I get that prickling feeling again. Taking a deep breath, I turn around and scour for the eyes that I know are on me. Again, I find nothing, but I continue to look, sliding past Mr Tattoo but apparently snagging his attention despite trying to avoid just that.

Our eyes meet yet again, only this time I can't look away. Like a moth drawn to a flame, I can't take my eyes off of him, and the longer I stare, the hotter I get. My blood is pounding, and my heart is pumping as one of his brows cocks smugly and he smirks, tipping a glass to his lips. Amber liquid sits in the bottom, whiskey, and after he's done, his tongue darts out to lap up any drops that are clinging to his lips.

"Uh, _who_ is that?" Vivi's spotted him.

I shrug and turn my attention back to the girls, "Who wants shots!?"

With a round of cheers, I climb from the table and head to the bar, my heels sticking to the floor, but I still somehow manage to get there without losing a shoe.

"Hey baby," a guy slides up next to me. "How you doing tonight?"

Rolling my eyes, I turn to the guy, taking in his thick blond hair and scruff on his jaw. He's a handsome guy. "No."

"Aw, come on, not even a dance?"

"Do you see anyone dancing?"

"I meant more of a private gig," he wags his eyebrows.

Seriously!?

"I'm gonna ask you a question," I turn myself fully towards him, straightening my spine, "Has that ever worked for you?"

He cocks his head to the side, "What do you mean?"

"Have you ever gone up to a chick in a bar and asked for a private dance and actually got one?"

"Well," he pauses, "No, I haven't."

"Maybe, instead of propositioning a woman in a bar you could offer to buy her a drink, give her your number, ask her out. If you actually want to get a woman, you're gonna need to treat her with a bit more respect."

He chews on his bottom lip, "You're right, I'm sorry."

I nod once, "It's fine but you're still not getting a dance."

He laughs, "Noted, can I buy you a drink?"

I sigh, "You know what…?"

"Ethan," he inserts.

"Ethan," I repeat, "Unless you want to buy a round of shots for four girls, I think you might want to sit this one out."

I jerk my head back to the three girls waiting for their shots and smirk when his eyes widen in that direction. I'm a little smug. I can at least admit we're a good-looking bunch, each with our own little quirks.

"I'll do it," he says eagerly.

I chuckle, "Then go right ahead, we'll take four fireball whiskeys."

Two

Zach

"Well shit man," West chuckles, "I can't believe you're actually here!"

I shake my head and tip my whiskey to my lips. It wasn't exactly by choice that I was here, we were opening an office here in LA and it needed someone experienced to oversee it. That would be me seeing as my brother was busy back in Seattle with HQ and his daughter. Wyatt Personal Security was our family business, handed down to the two of us after our father retired a few months back, though the LA office was planned long before that. It made sense to have an office here seeing as a shit ton of our business was in this city.

West and I went to college together and have been

friends since, it's actually nice to have someone here that I know. If not for him I'd probably be sitting in the condo, watching shit TV and eating pizza rather than eyeing a cute chick in a red dress.

I spotted her the moment she shoved her way through the bar, her curvaceous body weaving between the crowd. That dress, damn, it looks like it's been painted on, hugging every curve, every dip of her perfect body. Her long legs are tipped in black heels, the muscles of her calves defined and flexing with each step she takes. The sleeves fall off her shoulders, revealing her sharp collar bones and shoulders and I can see her tan lines, the pale stripes against her tanned skin.

Her deep brown hair is pulled up and away from her face, but she looks tense, her arched brows pulled down, vibrant blue eyes tired.

I've been watching her most of the night, subtly of course, well up until she finally looked at me from across the bar. She started off the night with just one friend, a cute little red head but then two others joined her.

"What's snagged your attention?" West asks, following my gaze.

I don't answer and my breath lodges in my throat as her gaze lands on mine. Before, she looked away quickly, but now, she holds my eyes, a muscle in her jaw ticking.

Someone says something and she jerks her attention away from me.

A loud cheer comes from the table a few seconds later and then red dress is getting up and making her way to the bar.

"Those girls," West whistles, "they're like works of art."

I turn my attention back to my friend, "You know them?"

He shakes his head and sips his beer, "Nah man, not really, they come in here often though."

Red dress is talking to a guy at the bar, but it doesn't look all that friendly. Her body is straight, and her hands are balled up into fists.

"Want another drink?" I ask West, finding an excuse to go up to the bar.

He nods so I hop down from my perch on the stool and head to the bar, settling myself a few yards down from her.

"Has that ever worked for you?" I hear her say.

"What can I get you?" The barman catches my attention and I don't hear the rest of the conversation as I order West and I drinks, when I finally tune back in there's a line of shots in front of her and she's walking back to the table, the same guy trailing behind like a lost fucking puppy.

Shit.

I make it back to the table with our drinks, but I can't help but watch the girls on the other side of the room, well red dress particularly.

"That one is Ray," West tells me.

"I thought you didn't know them," I say.

"I don't but everyone here knows their names," he shrugs, "The red head is Harper, the blonde one is Oli and she works here at the bar," he points out, "and the other is Vivian Prescott, the model."

I nod, recognising the model from the countless billboards she's posted on around the city.

"Go talk to them," West laughs like a kid in high school, "Nothing welcomes you to a new city like a warm body."

I'm not a shy guy. Shit, I've had my share of women over the years but there's something different about this one. Something that tells me I should be careful when approaching.

I scan the bar, noticing the several longing looks being thrown towards their table but it's one guy that really holds my attention. He sits at the bar, dressed in a pair of khaki pants and a blue shirt, his dark hair slicked back whilst he nurses a drink, clear liquid in a short glass, gin or vodka probably. His eyes are trained on their table, from here it looks like he's watching Vivian, the model, but I can't be sure.

A loud cheer comes from their table and I turn back, seeing them throw back their shots before slamming the empty glasses down onto the table.

Red dress – Ray as West so kindly pointed out, takes her hair from it's hold and it flows down her back in soft waves. Some of the tension she arrived with appears to have dissipated. The straggler she picked up at the bar has really tucked himself into them, sitting between the red head and the blonde, laughing along with their jokes and encouraging them as they order more shots and knock them back.

"Are they always like this?" I ask West.

He shrugs, "Nah, go talk to her man."

I glare at him. I really don't need encouragement when it comes to women. Call it arrogance or smugness or whatever the hell you want, I knew what to do with women. There hasn't been one that's said no to me yet and I highly doubt she'll be the first, not with the way her eyes heated when I gave her my signature smirk and quirked brow.

"I might just do that," I slam back my whiskey and make my way towards their table. I feel West watching me from behind and as I draw closer to the table, I actually feel a flutter in my stomach. What the fuck!? Am I nervous?

The red head – Harper – looks at me and her eyes go saucer wide, her mouth popping open with her drink halfway paused to her mouth.

"I just want someone to *rock* me," Ray is saying, oblivious to me, "You know, really rock me. I can honestly say I've never had a man make me orgasm."

I choke on my tongue.

Holy shit.

My blood heats and my heart pounds.

What the fuck was wrong with me!?

"Is that right?" I say, coming to a stop behind her. This close and even over the sickly aroma of alcohol and stale stench of sweat I can smell her perfume, citrusy and sweet.

Her whole body stiffens and oh so slowly, she turns to me, a blush creeping over her cheeks.

"Oh shit," she murmurs.

Pulling myself together I give her my signature grin and lean, placing my elbow on the back of the booth to look down on her.

I quickly look at each face on the table and nod in acknowledgement but my attention isn't off her for long.

"Hi," I smirk, "Can I get you a drink?"

I'm still stuck on the fact that apparently, she's never been given an orgasm. She looks maybe twenty four or five, how does one go that long without ever having an orgasm. I didn't like to brag – actually that's a lie, what man doesn't like to brag – but no woman has ever left my bed unsatisfied. She wants to be rocked? She just needs to come home with me.

I realise, whilst I've been taking in her face, the drape

of dark lashes around her electric blue eyes, her little pert nose and her full, painted, burgundy lips that put Cupid's bow to shame, she hasn't answered my question.

"Ray," one of the girls hisses at her.

I drag my gaze away from those lips and meet her eyes, cocking a brow in question.

"No." She answers finally.

I actually take a step back. Did she just say no?

"Uh, what?"

"No, I said no."

My eyes bounce around her face, fuck, she's stunning, with her high cheekbones and sharp jawline but I'm still stuck on that no.

"No?"

She nods, "No."

"Why?"

Okay, now I just sound desperate.

Turn around and walk away. Just do it.

"Because I said no," her words are slurred and ends in a little hiccup. She's a little tipsy, if not drunk. "Because," she continues, "And don't get me wrong, you're very attractive with this whole bad boy image you've got going on but you are bad news."

"You don't even know me," I defend.

She shrugs, "Don't need to."

Well hell. This isn't what I expected.

"I know your type," She continues.

"Raynie," I think it's Harper saying her name, "Ray stop!"

She ignores her friend.

"You're the type that wraps a girl like me round your little finger, dragging them along for a ride – I'm sure it's a great ride by the way – and then you break their heart at the end of it." She hiccups again, "And I'm not in the business of getting my heart broken, thank you very much. Dig the tattoos though."

I look to the faces on the table. Each one can't meet my eyes except the dude. He looks at me sympathetically and shrugs his shoulders.

This did not just happen.

Unable to just let it go, call it pride or whatever the fuck you like, I crouch down to her level. The woman was truly beautiful, every part of her, body, face, except maybe personality. "Thank you for your evaluation, it is much appreciated."

My tone is stony and cold.

Perhaps it's because she just embarrassed the fuck out of me and usually, I'm not this much of an asshole but to hell with it.

"You're right. I would have bought you a drink. I would have told you all the right things," My voice is low, low enough that her friends don't hear. I'm not a complete idiot. "I would tell you how special you are."

My words are lies, slipping off my tongue like acid.

"And then I'd take you home. I would peel this dress from your body and that orgasm you've never had?"

The heat in her eyes flares like wildfire.

"I would have given you plenty, I would have made you come on my tongue, fingers and cock," I grin, watching her pupils dilate to three times their size and her lips part on an exhale, "And then the next morning I would have kicked you from my bed and sent you on your way."

The shutters come down and that fire is put out.

Her blues narrow and her jaw clamps shut, "Asshole."

"Only living up to expectations." I stand from my

crouch, "Ladies," I nod to them and turn around, heading back to my table.

"What did he say!?" I hear one of the girls ask.

"I – I – I need to go." Ray stutters.

I grin. I can play the dickhead game just as well.

Three

Ray

Strong firm hands grip my inner thighs, pushing me apart and fire licks at my veins, turning my blood molten as it flows through my body. My head is thrown back, the column of my throat exposed as I push myself back into the pillows.

Those hands run up my legs and I feel his breath on my core, warmth spreading through me and pooling in my lower belly. I'm so hot for him its embarrassing. My hands reach out to tangle into that mess of soft black hair, bringing his mouth down onto the place that is pulsing for him.

A flick of his tongue against my clit has my back bowing off the bed but a hand, pressing to my stomach pushes me back down, holding me in place as his tongue tortures me.

Moonlight grey eyes meet mine as he looks up at me from his place between my legs and that hand that was holding me down snakes up my abdomen to capture a nipple between his fingers. I trace my eyes over the tattoos drawn into his skin and then the rumble of his voice causes all my muscles to clench.

"Come," he demands.

My orgasm has me darting up in bed, the sheets wrapped around my legs, my brow wet with sweat.

"Shit!" I hiss, "Shit!"

My bedroom door slams open and a sleep mused Harper stands in the doorway, a heavy baseball bat poised and ready to strike, "Where's the intruder!?"

I scoff and press a hand to my chest, feeling my heart beating erratically in my chest, "No intruder, Harp, we're good."

"I heard you calling out," she frowns, lowering the bat only a little as her eyes scan the room. "It sounded like you were being attacked!"

My cheeks warm with embarrassment. Did I really just have a wet dream? I really shouldn't be surprised, it's not the first one I've had since meeting *him*. No, he's had the starring role in my dreams for a while now.

I look back over to my best friend and shake my head. She may be socially awkward but she's fiercely protective, clearly fully prepared to break a skull to defend me.

It's been two weeks since that night in the bar and I haven't seen him since. Part of me hopes my subconscious is just exaggerating on how attractive he is but I know it's not. That man was a god. And I was a dick. A full-blown fucking asshole.

Fuck me and my stupid, drunk mouth.

"I'm good," I tell Harper, throwing myself back onto my pillows, "Bad dream."

"Oh," Harper lowers her bat, "Wanna talk about it?"

"No!" I say too quickly.

Harper narrows her eyes at me, "Well okay then, has it got something to do with these messages?"

I sigh, I had almost forgotten about that.

For the past two weeks Vivian has been overrun with strange messages. From one person in particular but always from different addresses.

They never name Vivi directly but they're coming into her personal inbox and they're disgusting.

They started off obsessive, telling her how beautiful she was, how *he*, I'm assuming he, but I can't be sure, wants to possess her, wants to touch her and tease her. Wants to *own* her. I ignored them at first but when they became more descriptive I notified Hudson, Vivian's manager and after that I had to report any new messages that came in.

This past week they've become violent.

Whoever this guy is he's hurt that she hasn't responded.

He promised that he'll find her and punish her for ignoring him. He declares that they are made for each other, that he's dreamed of her for years and they belong together.

It's all very creepy.

As Vivian's assistant, I see it all before she ever does which I'm thankful for. I can shield her from most of it so she never has to feel threatened but still, reading those messages, it makes me feel sick.

What was wrong with some people!?

"Yeah," I lie, instantly feeling guilty for using it as an excuse for my dream but shit, the girls gave me hell for how I treated that guy back at the bar that night and I really don't want to admit that I haven't managed to get him from my head.

'I would have made you come on my tongue, fingers and cock.'

I don't doubt it. He had this air about him that told me he knew what he was doing when it came to women.

No I definitely did the right thing even if I did it the wrong way. He was bad news, that much was true, and his little speech, one he spoke so purposely quiet so the others didn't hear, only cemented that fact.

I won't lie, hearing those rough words escape his lips, it lit a fire in me that hasn't been extinguished since. And that's ridiculous because he admitted he'd only use me for one reason but logic was non-existent when my mind conjured images of him.

"Oh hon," Harper crosses the room and sits on the edge of the bed, rubbing my arm soothingly, "It'll all be okay. Hudson has got a guy coming in tomorrow right?"

Ignoring my guilt I nod, "Yeah, some guy from a firm his buddy owns. I'm sure it'll make us all sleep better knowing Vivian is protected."

That much was true.

Things had been weird since the messages had started pouring in. Vivian was nervous to leave her house and even though she was driven everywhere she went, she was terrified she was being followed, always watched by this weirdo who keeps messaging her.

She's fairly new to the modelling scene and it's only been in the past few months that she's really taken off. Hudson had warned her that this kind of thing could happen but neither I nor Vivian actually expected it. I've worked with well established celebrities before and nothing like this has ever happened.

I mean sure, you get the die hard fans, declaring undying love for them and what not but nothing like this.

Nothing like the violence this guy is oozing into his words with vivid imagery.

Oli has been staying with Vivian the past few days to keep her company but tomorrow we'd meet the guy we've hired to be her personal security guard and hopefully it'll help her feel better. He will check over the security at her house, install anything required to keep her safe and well just protect her.

Hiring a guy was Hudson's idea but it was one I was well on board with. It was going to happen sooner or later with the way Vivian's popularity was sky rocketing so there's no time like the present.

"Well that's good," Harper continues, "We'll all sleep better."

I nod my agreement, "Thanks for checking on me."

She smiles, "Anytime."

And with that, she fully lowers the bat, puts it back in its position in the living room – we're two females living alone and we have to protect ourselves – and goes back to bed.

I drop back down onto my pillows and let out a long breath.

With that dream still lingering around inside my brain there's no way I'll be able to sleep. I pull my phone from its charging port and start scrolling through tomorrows schedule.

Nine A.M. meet Hudson at Aurora Modelling.

Nine Fifteen, Vivian to be at office for run down.

Nine Thirty, Personal Security arriving.

After that it would be a rush to get Vivian down to the studio to start preparations for the music video she's shooting. Yes, she was chosen for the music video with Nate Sandford and then after that she was to be at an interview with a local radio station. It would be a busy day and I really needed to get some sleep.

I was always busy with this job. It wasn't just running behind Vivian, it was making sure she had everything she needed, it was time management and organisation. Without me, I highly doubted she'd be able to tell her ass from her elbow and that's got nothing to do with her own personal management but she has so much on her plate, I'm here to help her fit it into all the right holes.

I loved my job.

I loved that my boss was also one of my best friends, I loved that it kept me busy and I got to meet some amazing people. I've been places people have only dreamed about. I get to see things that people don't even realise are real and I get paid really well.

Harper and I live together in a nice apartment that overlooks the beach, there's a balcony off of the kitchen that gives a perfect view of the sandy beaches and rolling waves. In my downtime, when I'm not with the girls or visiting my family, I'm down on that very beach either lapping up the sunshine or on the water with my paddle board.

I've always loved the water so being this close keeps my heart at ease.

Unable to shut off, I climb from the bed and pad through the dark apartment.

Harper's door is closed and I can hear the faint sound of the music she listens to, to get herself to sleep drifting beneath the door. I make myself a camomile tea and then slip out onto the balcony, sliding the glass door closed behind me.

The city is still awake beneath me but it is LA so it never really sleeps. Bright yellow cabs drive the desolate streets seven floors beneath me but other than that, the roads are empty. Loud laughs and banter travel through the streets, echoing down the empty alleys after late night revelers make their way home but above all of that, I can hear the waves.

I can hear the water hitting the sand as it rolls and between the high rises ahead of me, I can make out the glow of the moon hitting the water and reflecting back off the waves.

The colour reminds me of the tattooed guy. I didn't even get his name, something I now regret but I bet it's something edgy and cool, something that matches his exterior, all bad and confident.

I can't even lie and say I wasn't attracted to him. I was, so fiercely attracted it actually scared me. It was almost primal, natural the way my body lit up at his nearness, at the scent of him, a mix of whiskey on his breath and sandalwood with a hint of something smoky. I wanted to explore those tattoos. I wanted to see how far they went, did they disappear under the caps of his sleeves and worm over his chest and go further than that? Where did they stop? Could I trace them with my fingertip?

Goose bumps chase over my skin as I think about him, at the way his eyes ate me up whilst he gazed down at me. Fuck he was so perfect.

His black tee stretched over his muscular torso like a second skin and his arms were firm, the muscle well defined.

His eyes could rival the moon, truly, with the way they stood out in comparison to his olive complexion and dark hair. His lashes framed them like a lover would, and a dusting of dark stubble lined his granite jaw line. The hollows beneath his high cheekbones were deep, accentuating his delicious bone structure and that mouth! Jeez, that mouth looked like it knew what it was doing. Pillowy and soft, waiting to be kissed and touched and teased.

I squirm in my seat on the balcony and then take a sip of the tea that claims to calm you.

I don't feel calm. Not even a little. I just feel flustered and nervous and antsy. I have no idea what tomorrow will bring and with my mind preoccupied with images of a man I'm never going to see again, I feel like I'm missing something.

Something incredibly important but whilst it's there, it's hidden by a wall I can't bring down.

I just hope whatever it is isn't so important that it puts someone in danger.

Four

Ray

I'm barely functional when I wake the next morning at six A.M. and I'm sure I'm so tired I'd use the cascading water in the shower as a grip should I slip and fall.

I run my hands over my face and rub my eyes, trying to scrub away the fatigue. I really did try to get back to sleep but my dreams were haunted by his face and that, mixed with the messages, makes for one tired, grumpy Ray this Monday morning.

I pour my coffee into my favourite travel mug, grinning when I read the caption scrolled into the side of the pink mug in gold lettering – *Of course size matters. No one likes a small coffee.*

I tended to agree with it.

Nobody's got time for a small coffee. What's the point if it doesn't get you buzzed?

Harper trudges out of her bedroom, red hair resembling some sort of birds nest just as I'm preparing to leave for the day.

"Hey," she mumbles, pouring a coffee for herself. "Good luck today."

I smile, "May your day go fast and your coffee cup never go empty."

She nods and smiles at our mantra, "Have a good day."

I wave my goodbyes and press the bell for the elevator, clutching my coffee to my chest.

As I enter, my cell buzzes with a new message and I'm pulling it out as the metal doors close behind me.

Good morning.

It is a beautiful morning today, the sun is truly shining, just like my love for you.

We are made for each other, I know it, and soon you will too.

I hope your day goes as well for you today as I know mine will for me.

Until we meet officially.

Yours forever.

I cringe and pocket my phone. It's never signed off with a name or alias and always from a different email address.

When I make it to the onsite parking lot I find my little mini cooper and climb in behind the wheel, quickly forwarding the email over to Hudson. It's a short drive through the city to the Aurora offices and when I park, I notice Hudson's Mercedes parked at the front of the building.

I drag myself through the lot and up to the twentieth floor, finding Vivian's manager tucked behind his desk on the phone.

"Yes, yes," Hudson says, his dark eyes flicking to me as I enter the office, "I'll see you shortly."

He hangs up and scrubs a hand down his face, his eyes scanning the laptop in front of him.

"You get this shit this morning?" He asks.

I nod, "Bright and early."

"This dude is seriously whacko."

I laugh, "You're telling me!"

He shakes his head, "We're going to have to involve the cops eventually, I know it."

I purse my lips. Vivian was clear in her wishes not to involve the authorities. I'm not sure why but I think it's got something to do with publicity.

She's not had the easiest time with the press with most questioning *why* she managed to get a deal in the first place which is completely ridiculous. The girl is stunning but she's not tall like a model would be and came from real humble backgrounds.

"I know," I say on a sigh, "Let's just see what happens. Maybe the guy will back off when they see the security we've hired."

Hudson shrugs, "Maybe."

"And you have no idea who it could be?" I quiz again.

I'd read somewhere the person 'stalking' is likely to be known to the victim.

Hudson shakes his head, "No idea."

We discuss Vivian's schedule for the day before she turns up a short time later. She slumps down into the chair next to me, her dark hair tied up in a high bun, her body dressed in low hanging sweats and a tight tank. She slurps at a takeaway coffee.

"Please tell me this shit is over with," she grumbles.

Hudson smiles sympathetically, "No, unfortunately not."

I study him. I've known the man for quite some time now. His blonde hair is cropped short at the sides but longer at the top, a mixture of honey and gold. His eyes are dark brown but almost black and his face is handsome, in a preppy, boy next door kind of way. It's no secret he pushed himself to the top, becoming a manager fairly quickly in the game but he cares deeply for his models, Vivian being his main. We get along really well.

"How are you feeling about it all, Vivi?" I ask.

She shrugs, "I don't know really. A little freaked."

"That's understandable," Hudson nods, "Hopefully getting you a bodyguard will ease some of that."

She visibly shivers, "I hate that."

I'm not able to hide my laugh, "Like you hated having me around?"

"Exactly," she clicks her fingers.

I roll my eyes and pull my iPad from my bag, going through the schedule again for today. We're still on time which is a first for us, just as long as the guy Hudson hired turns up on time.

I'm still looking through the tablet when a knock on the office door snags my attention. Ignoring it, I stare down at my pad, memorising the times to make sure I don't forget anything.

"Oh my God." Vivian whisper shouts in my ear, "Get the fuck off that tablet!"

My head snaps up at her tone, "Excuse me!?"

She's never spoken to me that way before.

"Be offended later," she snatches the tablet from my hands, "Look who just fucking walked through the door!"

"What the hell are you talking about!?" I hiss back, sitting up in my chair to look behind me.

My heart stops.

Dead.

I'm gone.

Oh no.

Hudson stands from behind his desk but I can't stop staring at the man who's just walked through the door.

He looks different now that he's dressed for work but I'd never forget those eyes, or that face for that matter.

He's dressed in a black suit today with a white shirt but no tie. Tattoos hidden under that professional exterior. His hair is still purposely messy, soft black in colour and when his eyes meet mine over Hudson's shoulder all I see is amusement.

"Oh fuck," I blurt.

"It's him isn't it?" Vivian whispers, "The guy from

the bar?"

I nod, "Yeah, that's him alright."

"This just got really interesting," Vivian chuckles lightly.

"This is a disaster," I whine.

"No," Vivi laughs, "This is just what I need to keep my mind off the weirdo stalking me. It's like a sitcom, just get me some popcorn and I'll settle right in."

"I doubt he even remembers me," *not like I remember him anyway.*

"Oh, he remembers you," she laughs, "Look at the way he's looking at you. That's full on alpha male right there. Oh, it's giving me tingles. You're gonna make beautiful babies."

I snap me head back to her, "What the hell!?"

"You're not the only one Harper lends books to," She shrugs, "I know how this ends."

"Oh please," I scoff, "You're being ridiculous."

She shrugs with a grin, "If you say so."

"I do say so" I snap.

She just laughs, leaning back in her chair and kicking her legs over the arm, like she's settling in to watch the show.

Oh fuck. This is not good.

Not good at all.

Hudson walks the guy over to us, "Vivian, this is Zach Wyatt, your new personal security."

Dread settles into me. I guess part of me was hoping this was something else but nope, he's here to do and be, exactly what I was hoping he wouldn't be.

"Zach, this is Raynie, or Ray, Vivian's assistant, I'm sure you two will work quite closely together in the future."

God no.

"Oh, I'm sure they'll be working closely," Vivian agrees, "Hi Zach, I'm Vivian, we've already met I believe."

"That we have," the deep timbre of his voice cuts right through me and I swallow, closing my eyes as the vibration of it ricochets through my body.

"Ray, are you going to say hello?"

Right. I'm just standing here with my eyes closed and not saying anything.

I spin on my heels, almost losing my balance and face the man that's been the permanent star of my dreams since I met him, "Hi, I'm Ray."

"Zach Wyatt," he holds out a hand and etiquette tells me to take it, but I really don't want to. My fingers curl in, tightening until my nails dig into my palms but then politeness wins out and I reach forward to take his hand.

A shot of electricity shoots up my arm and I snatch my hand back, cradling it against my chest like he'd burned me.

He smirks arrogantly and turns his attention back to Hudson, "So, I hear you've had a bit of trouble."

Five

Zach

Her sweet scent invades my nose and her heat brushes against my skin. She's as rigid as a board, her shoulders bunched up around her ears and her jaw clamped tight. I can see a tremor in her hand as she scrolls through the countless emails from Vivian's new admirer.

"He's very persistent," she tells me, her voice small with a shake.

I stifle my amusement. Seeing the way those big blues widened when she saw me was priceless. Did I know I would be seeing her today? Of course I fucking did.

When Vivian's name popped up in my email I decided to give them the personal treatment. Raynie Stone had been on my mind since that night back at the bar and whilst it's completely childish of me, I wanted to fuck with her some more.

Sure, I could have got one of my other guys on it but what would be the fun in that?

"This is the first threatening message we received," Ray tells me, handing me the tablet.

It's not very nice to ignore people, little bird.
Why aren't you emailing me back?
You're going to find out real soon just who I am and then you will realise how much we belong together.
I'm afraid I will have to punish you for the ignorance but don't worry, little bird, it won't hurt too much.
Until we see each other.

I've dealt with stalkers before, this one is no different and most of the time they're all mouth. I flick between the email addresses, each one different from the last. I send all the emails over to our IT department and type out a message.

"What are you doing?"

"Sending it to my IT guy, he might be able to get a tag on the IP address."

Ray nods, pulling her bottom lip between her teeth.

"Are you nervous, sweetheart?" I ask in a low voice. Hudson and Vivian are busy talking in the corner meaning we have a semblance of privacy.

"No," she snaps, "Why would I be nervous?"

"Oh, I don't know," I grin, "But with the way you're shaking, one would think my presence is affecting you."

"God you're an asshole," she hisses, her eyes flicking to Hudson to make sure he didn't hear her, "You're here to do a job, you and I, we don't have to have anything to do with each other outside of work."

"You've thought about it haven't you," God knows I have, "About what I said back at the bar."

"Oh please," she scoffs, "You're hardly memorable."

Oh. Ouch. She's got some claws on her. Little did she know a little bit of fire in a girl will only spur me on more.

She looks at her watch, "Time to go."

Without another word she spins on her heels and struts over to Vivian, her face softening at the model. I take a quick second to appreciate her body, dressed in a tight beige skirt that hits her knees and light pink blouse that's tucked in at the waist. The thin material stretches over her ample breasts but it's not low cut so she's completely hidden. I like a woman who doesn't show off too much, it lets my imagination run a little. With her feet in a pair of light pink stilettos to match that blouse, she's a picture of office elegance.

She really does have a cracking set of legs and when I eventually get her in bed, because I will, I'm going to make her way those heels.

Scrubbing a hand across the scruff on my jaw I join them, plucking up my keys from the table.

"Ready, ladies?" I ask, looking only at Ray and taking far too much pleasure out of the way she squirms beneath my gaze.

"As we'll ever be," Vivian answers for the both of them. Reluctantly, I drag my eyes from Ray to look at the model. She's not like the other models I've worked with, for one, she seems completely down to earth and friendly. With her long light brown hair pulled into a high bun and her lithe body dressed in sweats and a tank, she oozes a girl next door vibe. She has a sweet face, her dark eyes are doe like, framed by thick lashes and she has a pouty pink mouth.

She's definitely beautiful but Ray – fuck, now that woman was gorgeous.

They say their goodbyes to Hudson and then I'm following them out of the office and through the building. People have started to filter in now, ready to start the working day and a couple of heads turn our way.

Ray makes a disgruntled noise in the back of her throat whilst Vivian chuckles, throwing a look over her shoulder. I'm assuming they're discussing the numerous women looking our – my – way and I smirk.

When we enter the elevator, Ray presses herself into the corner and stares down at the tablet in her hand, never once lifting her gaze to me even though I know she can tell I'm looking at her.

I should probably back off a bit, really I know that but this is too much fun.

"So, Zach," Vivian speaks up, "Where are you from?"

"Seattle," I answer, "We've just opened an office here in LA."

"Your last name is Wyatt, right? So Wyatt Personal Security is your company?"

Vivian nudges Ray with her elbow but the woman barely acknowledges it. She's focused on that damn device in her hands. I'll give it to her, she's as stubborn as a mule. It'll be fun breaking her.

"I co own it with my brother, he's back in Seattle."

"That's nice," Vivian says, "Isn't it, Ray?"

She grunts.

"You know, I don't think your *assistant*, likes me very much." I say assistant rather than friend because I know it'll piss her off.

And just as I expected her eyes finally lift from the pad and flare at me, anger brightening the blues like lightning.

The metal doors slide open and Ray storms out,

heading out into the early morning sunshine and turning left on the sidewalk rather than right where my SUV is parked. Both Vivian and I stop to watch her, her hips bouncing from left to right.

"You know what," Vivian laughs, "You're right. She doesn't like you much at all."

"She will," I answer quietly, "You wanna go get her? My car is that way."

"I wouldn't piss her off too much," Vivian warns, "She holds a grudge and I'm not going to lie, she can be a little scary."

I laugh, "See you back at the car."

Vivian hurries after Ray as I turn and unlock the car with the button. The lights flash twice and I stand by the door, waiting for the girls.

Ray's cheeks are burning red when she makes it back and she refuses to meet me in the eye, instead she throws herself into the back of the car and proceeds to tap away at the tablet. "Address has been sent to you," she spits.

Vivian cocks a brow and climbs in after her.

—

I pull up at the studio and put the SUV in park. Before I can get out and open the door for Ray, she's already climbing out, storming off to wait by the door.

For the rest of the day she ignores me, placing herself at least fifty yards away from me at every point. I don't try to start a conversation with her, giving her space. Instead I watch the people around the building.

No one stands out. There isn't anyone lingering at the edges of the rooms we're in, no weird fans shouting or screaming when Vivian steps from each building we find ourselves in. It's all completely normal.

Having spent years in this business I've learned a lot

about people. I've had to fight off mobs of fans and with every other stalker I've dealt with, they've always shown up. They're sketchy and jumpy, sticking to the edges of the crowds to watch or they're in your face, trying like hell to get your attention but nothing like that happens with Vivian.

It would be unlikely that whoever this is hasn't shown up today. It's an addiction to them, a need to be near that person they're currently obsessing over and without them, they'd experience what could be known as withdrawal.

After we leave a radio station, I stand close behind Vivian, using my body as a shield from the crowd that had gathered outside. She tucks herself in close, but she doesn't appear afraid. Ray however, has gone pale and I can't tell if it's because of the crowd or whatever it is she's looking at on her pad.

I don't press, I guide both women into the back of the car and climb up front.

"Where to now?" I ask.

"That's our day done with I think," Vivian says, nudging Ray.

Ray looks up, a frown marring her brow and then she nods, "Uh, yes, all done."

"Could you drop me home?" Vivian asks me, "I got a cab this morning."

"Sure," I say, "You need to avoid getting public transport now, call me or a driver when you need to get somewhere. I'll be with you most of the time so it shouldn't be a problem, I'd also like to have a quick look around your place, we might need to add a bit more security."

"Sure," Vivian answers, "That okay with you Ray?"

"Mm," Ray mumbles, her thumb nail between her

teeth.

I meet her eyes in the rear-view mirror, a question in my eyes but she ignores me, proceeding to stare out the window, watching the concrete jungle roll on by.

I pull up to Vivian's apartment building and follow her inside, Ray following a few steps behind me. There's a concierge so I tell the girls to wait as I go over to speak with him.

"Hey man," I offer a hand, "I'm Zach, Vivian's personal security, mind if I ask you a few questions?"

The middle-aged guy nods and sits up straighter, darting a look over my shoulder, "Sure, everything okay?"

I shrug, "A little bit of trouble," I answer honestly, "Do people have to come through you when entering this building?"

"Yes, sir," he nods, "I have a list of approved guests but anyone not on the list has to wait here whilst I contact the resident. We ask for photo ID and they can't get in the elevator without the guest code."

I nod my approval, "I assume that changes on a daily basis?"

"Yes sir."

"Good, that's good. What's your name?"

"Thomas, sir," he answers, looking back to the girls.

"You know them?"

"Very well, they're good girls. Who's causing trouble?"

"Unsure yet, man, but it's good to know there's people to look out for them."

"Anytime," he nods. I say my goodbyes and make my way back to the girls. "Let's go."

Vivian punches in her code and we climb into the small cart. It's so small Ray has no choice but to touch me. Her bare arm brushes the sleeve of my suit jacket and no matter how much she tries to shuffle away from me she can't escape. At Vivian's floor, Vivian skips out but before Ray can escape, I lean down and whisper in her ear, "Unfortunately, sweetheart, you can't run away from me."

Goose bumps erupt on her skin but she doesn't respond like I expect her to, instead she glares at me and then heads out.

Vivian's apartment is modest, three bedrooms with an open plan living room and kitchen and with it being so high up the building I don't have to worry about someone breaking in via a window. There's a security panel at the door and an intercom. It would take some real work to be able to get into this place.

Satisfied I say my goodbyes and both Ray and I leave. I finally have her to myself and I grin, wondering just how much I can rile her up in the time it takes us to get back to the office.

Six

Ray

Just don't look at him. It's easy. Stare at your very pretty shoes and think unsexy things.

Hating him and wanting him all at the same times is very confusing. It's like this internal war I'm having with myself and it makes me do weird things.

I look back down at the tablet, getting a cold slap when the email loads up again. I really need to tell Zach about it but that smug look on his face is really pissing me off.

No, this is Vivian's safety we're talking about here, I have to tell him even if talking to him is the last thing I want to do.

Instead of saying anything, I shove the tablet in his direction once the elevator doors close. I press myself into the corner and hold my breath. Being enclosed in a small space with this man should come with a warning. It's like he gives off a vibe, one that makes my muscles clench with need and heat pool low in my belly. He smells so God damned good it should be a crime to smell so appealing.

I watch his face as he reads the very simple email I received a few hours ago.

I see you. It read. *You look so good. Who is that man you are with? I see the way he looks at you. You need to tell him to back off before I do something we both will regret.*

"He was with us?" Zach grumbles, more to himself and then shakes his head.

I hadn't noticed him looking at Vivian today but then I was so focused on not looking at him that I probably wouldn't have seen it anyway. I shouldn't feel jealous. I shouldn't and yet the way my stomach churns with unease can only be described as envy which is completely ridiculous. I don't want the man. He's an asshole.

I'd really like to say the whole alpha male thing he's got going on puts me off, but I can't deny it. I suppose it's only natural, right? The guy is a walking tank, all muscle and confidence. There's an air about him, a force that can't be ignored. That's why I'm attracted to him, it has to be. This just goes back to time of cavemen and how the woman chooses a male that can provide.

If there is one thing about Zach I'm sure of, it's that he can provide. Probably in more ways than one.

Just look at those hands, big and firm and – *no!* stop it! I squeeze my eyes closed.

Think unsexy thoughts!

"I didn't notice anyone," Zach says, louder this time.

Right he's talking to me.

"Me either," I wouldn't have noticed anything to be

honest.

I wave to Thomas on the way out and head to Zach's SUV, ready to climb into the back seat.

"Sit upfront," He says.

I spin around to me, "The back is fine."

He opens the passenger door and waits patiently for me to climb in.

"I don't bite," he tells me with a grin.

"I do," I huff back.

"Oh," he chuckles, "That sounds like fun. Your place or mine?"

"You're such a pig!" I growl before he slams the door. He's still chuckling to himself when he climbs behind the wheel.

I need a stiff drink, anything to take away the tension that's coiled my muscles tight. With everything going on I really don't need him adding to my already overflowing plate.

He presses a few buttons on the radio and music starts to play through the speakers and before he pulls away, he unhooks a few buttons at the collar of his shirt. My eyes are drawn to the golden skin revealed at his throat, showing off those sexy collar bones – no idea when I suddenly found clavicles sexy – and a slither of ink peeking out the edges. My mouth waters and I have to grip the door handle, pushing down the need to strip him from that shirt to explore his body.

He's infuriating but damn, infuriating never looked so good!

The drive back to the office is tense and silent. He doesn't try to tease me or make conversation which I suppose I should be thankful for but I'm not sure I like this silence. It's heavy, like there's something waiting just around the corner and you're expecting it but it's still going to surprise you when it's dropped in your lap.

"We'll figure it out," Zach says eventually as we're pulling up to the building, he must have taken my tense silence as worry which of course, I am, but in his presence I have a hard time thinking about much else.

"I know," I reply and escape the car as soon as he stops.

"See you tomorrow!" He yells at me, amusement lacing his tone.

I wave a dismissive hand and climb into the safety of my car. Thankfully, the air is untainted by Zach inside and I inhale a calming breath. I head straight home and find Harper sat in our little book hole we installed between the massive bookcases in the living room. Her glasses are perched on her nose and her headphones are placed over her ears. She's hasn't heard me come in, too engrossed in the book she's reading.

Instead of disturbing her, I head through to my bedroom, strip from my clothes and pull on an oversized tee that reads, *That sounds like a terrible idea. What time?* And a pair of shorts. I scrub my face free of makeup but even though I'm in my comfy clothes I feel all pent up.

Working with Zach was going to be hard.

I wasn't sure what was going to happen, would I strangle him or straddle him? Your guess is as good as mine, but the mere thought of *straddling* Zach had heat pooling between my thighs. This is not healthy, lusting after an arrogant asshole like that would be very bad for my wellbeing.

Knowing that however doesn't stop my dreams that night being all about him. According to my subconscious, it likes him in a suit and my mind has conjured up images of him dressed in low hanging black slacks, his shirt unbuttoned and untucked, revealing rippled abs and that delicious V that makes even the smartest of women lose a few brain cells. His mouth is cocked in a smirk, his eyes alight with amusement as he finally has his way with me.

The following day I'm so tired I can hardly think straight.

"Coffee?" I grumble as Harper bounces out of her bedroom, far too peppy for this early in the morning.

Today is the day Vivian is shooting the music video with Nate Sandford and I really need to be on point for this.

"Yes, please," Harper replies and I grab a mug from the draining board, drying it with a towel.

"I didn't see you last night," Harper says, settling in at the kitchen table with her phone and keys.

"Went straight to bed," I shrug, stifling yet another yawn.

"Vivian text me, I heard Zach's her new bodyguard."

Hearing his name just brings the dreams circling back round and, in my haste to change the subject, instead of throwing the towel onto the kitchen counter I launch the mug at the side. It shatters and shards of porcelain scatter over the counter.

"Fuck!" I yell.

"Right, well noted, don't mention Zach."

"Sorry!" I exclaim, "I didn't sleep well."

"We should go out at the weekend," Harper says, changing the subject, "All of us. We haven't been out since that night at Franks."

That could be just what I need. After cleaning up the side and handing Harper a fresh mug of coffee I pick up my travel mug and say my goodbyes. Harper's on the planning for the night out on Friday and I'm vowing not to let Zach get to me.

I mean I hardly know him, he really shouldn't have this much control over my emotions.

I'll apologise for my outburst at him back at Franks and then hopefully we can just proceed without all the teasing and taunting. We can be grown ups about this.

I'm nodding to myself as I make my way over to Vivian's. That's a solid plan.

Thomas waves at me as I walk through the door. I'm here so often I have my own code for the elevators so don't need to stop and get a code.

I unlock the front door with my spare key, calling out Vivian's name as I walk through.

As I wait for her to come out of the bedroom, I pull out the tablet, noting I haven't had any new messages this morning. That's a first.

"Good morning, sunshine," Vivian beams as she meets me in the kitchen, "And how are you? Did you and Zach get it on last night?"

I groan, "Give it up. That's never going to happen."

She scoffs, "Oh please the chemistry between the two of you is so hot it could catch fire."

I roll my eyes, "Behave. You ready for today?"

"Yes," She breathes, "I get to get all cosy with Nate Sandford, of course I'm ready." She shimmies her shoulders a little, a playful smile tugging on her mouth.

"Well Zach," I swallow, "should be here soon."

"You know what," she taps her manicured finger against her bottom lip, "If you're not interested, I might give him a go, I mean the man is a fine piece of work to look at. Do you reckon he'd tangle with a client?"

Heat flares through my veins, "What!?" I snap. "Are you serious?"

She smiles knowingly, "Well I mean, if you mind, then you can have him."

I narrow my eyes at her, "I'm not playing this game with you. He's not a toy you can pass around."

"Why, Ray, that sounds like you're defending him or maybe it's a little jealousy?"

"I am not jealous." I grit my teeth, "Have him if you want him."

The words taste foul on my tongue. I'd never admit that though.

"Nah," she sighs, "Don't get me wrong, he's hot as sin but not really my type."

"Then why say it?"

"Because it was fun watching you get all riled up," she giggles, "You're so stubborn sometimes but when you want something, you'll do anything to get it and you want Zach. I know it."

"I do not."

She shrugs delicately just as the intercom buzzes and Thomas's voice sounds through the speaker, "A one Mr Zach Wyatt is here to collect you, Miss Prescott, should I send him up?"

She skips over to the buzzer, "Send him up, Thomas. Thank you."

"Very well, Miss Prescott."

"I just need to grab a few more things," Vivian tells me, "Let him in when he gets here."

I'm still grumbling to myself when there's a knock on the door. Reluctantly I trudge to the door and throw it open.

I'm fully aware of what he looks like, I know what he smells like and yet, seeing him in the doorway, taking up the entire frame with his sheer size my breath still lodges in my throat and I'm pretty sure I just squeaked.

"Well good morning, sweetheart," he grins, his eyes raking down my body. I'm dressed in a tight cobalt blue dress today, one that fits every curve like a second skin and my heels are white, "Don't you just look good enough to eat."

"In your dreams," I hiss and then chastise myself. Be nice, Ray.

"Every night, sweetheart," he chuckles as he brushes past me and into the apartment but I'm too stumped to move.

Did he really just admit to dreaming about me?

Yes. Yes he did.

Seven

Ray

I feel his eyes on me as I walk into the studio, following a very pepped up Vivian who's buzzing with so much excitement it's palpable.

I spin back to Zach, letting Vivian go ahead, "We need to work this out."

He grins, "I have my ways," he cocks a brow, "What do you suggest sweetheart?"

"Well first," I bristle, "You can stop with the *sweetheart*."

"Why's that?"

He's so smug and arrogant the apology I have on tip of my tongue gets swallowed right back down.

"Forget it," I storm off, finding Vivian waiting by the reception area of the studio. We sign in and head through the long halls to a dressing room where a team of hair and makeup artists are waiting.

Zach waits in the hall as the team get to work on

Vivian, curling her long hair and applying a light, natural layer of makeup.

An hour or so later and we're heading towards another section.

I've been to plenty of studios before, it's nothing new so whilst Vivian is taking the tour with the producer, I head down to the refreshment table to get a coffee, revelling in the silence. With Zach having to follow Vivian around I can actually think without the stench of testosterone invading my senses.

I take my first sip and groan. God that's good.

Coffee in hand I head over to the sofas and settle in. They'll be a little while so I can get some of the admin I'd been putting off done.

My alone time doesn't last long. The sofa dips next to me but I keep my eyes down, if I don't acknowledge them maybe whoever it is will leave me alone.

A few seconds drag by and then whoever it is clears their throat, "Hi."

With a long exhale I close down the tablet and turn to face them, "Can I help you?"

I'm met with a familiar face but I can't quite place it. I'm sure I've seen him before though. A mess of dark hair, copper in places and a cute face, boyish almost. He's cleanly shaven and has a little cleft in the middle of his chin. His blue eyes are smiling.

"Sorry," I smile, "Do I know you?"

His brows twitch as if wanting to pull into frown, but he smooths his features quickly, "Yeah, we met a few weeks back, I was the photographer for that fashion shoot with Vivian."

I click my fingers. That's right, "Oh hi! Sorry, I'm a mess when it comes to names."

"Oh that's okay, Sam," he holds a hand out and I take

it.

"Ray," I introduce.

"I know," he grins, holding onto my hand far too long for my liking. I tug until he finally relents and then hide it in my lap. "I'm shooting the stills for the video." He informs.

I don't like the way he's studying my face and he's edged closer on the couch.

"Sorry Sam," I pick up my tablet, "It was nice chatting but I've got to get on."

"You're quite busy as an assistant then? Does she have you running all over the place?"

"Um no," I turn my back a little, hoping if I show a cold shoulder he'll take the hint.

I feel him edge closer still.

"You're real pretty, maybe I can take you out sometime?"

His finger purposely brushes the outside of the knee closest to him and a chill runs through me. I snatch my knee away so hard it bashes against the other one. Wincing, I glare at him. That's going to leave a bruise.

"I'm not dating anyone at the moment."

Something in me is screaming to abort. Now. Escape.

"Good, that's good," he tries to touch me again.

"I mean, I'm not dating. I don't want to date and have no plans to anytime soon."

If I get up and run now, do you think people would think I was strange?

He reaches forward and grips my knee before I can snatch it away from him. "Maybe you can make an exception for me, hmm?"

I stand abruptly, knocking the table in front of me. My coffee spills over the rim and onto a bunch of paperwork someone had left there.

"Don't touch me!" I shriek.

Jesus Christ! What the hell was wrong with people!?

"What's going on here?" I've never been so happy to hear Zach's voice.

He's behind me and for whatever reason I step back into him, feeling his chest against my back. His hand curls around my shoulder and he squeezes reassuringly.

"Who are you?" Sam barks, eyes narrowing in on the hand on my shoulder. "She told me she wasn't dating anyone."

"I'm not," I hiss, "But it's none of your god damn business!"

We've gathered the attention of a few others now and they're watching the scene, hushed whispers passing between them. I don't care if I have to scream it. This fucking guy needs to leave.

"I think there may be a misunderstanding here, we're friends aren't we, Ray," Sam declares.

"No. We're not friends."

A flash of anger flicks across his face but he quickly shoves it back down and then smiles, "I can see when I should make an exit."

"That's right," Zach growls, "Off you fuck."

His hand is still squeezing my shoulder but now his thumb is circling almost soothingly. If I didn't feel the menace radiating off of him, I'd actually relax into his hold.

I watch with bated breath as Sam turns to leave, looking back once before slamming his way out the door and disappearing.

"Are you okay?" Zach's voice is a whisper into the shell of my ear.

No. No I am not okay. And it has nothing to do with that Sam guy. Oh no, it has everything to do with the man still pressed up against my back, his hand still on my shoulder.

Oh, I'm in so much trouble.

Eight

Zach

"Are you okay?" I whisper into her ear. She's still pressed into me, the curve of her ass pressing into my hips and her back against my chest. I really need to let her go, remove my hand from her shoulder and check he didn't hurt her.

I'm not even going to deny the anger that swarmed when I saw that guy touch her. Clearly, she didn't want him to and that was only backed up by the fact that she stood so abruptly she knocked the table in front of her.

I'd seen that guy before, but I can't place where. His face, it was familiar somehow but that's the least of my worries as Ray quakes under my hand.

"Hey, hey," I soothe, guiding her back to the couch and gently pushing her down to sit, "Did he hurt you?"

She shakes her head.

"What then? What's wrong?"

"Just a little," she waves her hand, "Spooked."

"Understandable," I tell her, crouching in front of her and handing her, her coffee, "Want to talk about it?" I search her face, losing myself a little in the blue of her eyes.

"Not with you."

And there it is.

I bristle, "Oh that's right." I stand, stepping out of her space, more for me than her, "I'm bad news."

"Shit," she winces, "Zach wait, I'm–"

"Forget it," I cut her off and before she can say anything else I spin on my heel and head back to where I left Vivian with the producer.

"Zach!" I hear her yell but she's not chasing me so it can't be that important.

I stay on the side-lines for the rest of the day, keeping my distance from Ray and watching Vivian like a hawk. She's getting real cosy with that singer, even off film they're laughing and chatting like they've been friends for years. Ray tried to talk once or twice but each time I ignored her until she was little ball of fury and her pride won. Both occasions she cussed me out and stormed off.

Truth be told, I didn't like that she had somehow gotten under my skin. It wasn't just the rejection in the bar, I mean I can take no for an answer it's the fact that despite it all, and despite her animosity, I'm still ridiculously attracted to the girl. Her curves, her eyes, her smart mouth, all of it just leaves me wanting more. Call me a sadist, having her fire aimed at me got me hotter than the sun and I really had to start questioning my sanity.

At the end of the day I drop both girls at Vivian's apartment, seeing them in through the doors and watching them disappear in the elevator before I head back to my condo. I text West earlier today to meet for drinks but first I need to shower and get through some emails I've neglected the last couple of days.

By nine I'm showered, dressed and heading back out, opting to take my bike rather than the SUV. I pull my helmet over my head and straddle the machine, feeling the purr of the engine between my legs.

Franks is busy when I pull up and park, I notice West's Jag is already parked out front. I head in through the doors, spotting him immediately with a woman hanging off his arm.

"Hey man," I slap his shoulder and settle on the stool, cocking my brow at the chick.

"See you later, honey," West drawls, earning a high pitched giggle from the girl and he watches her as she sashays away. "What's up, Zach?"

I grab the attention of a server and order a beer, keeping it light seeing as I'm riding tonight and then scrub a hand down my face.

"So," I start, "I may or may not have accepted a job that put me in the same room as Ray."

"You're shitting me."

I laugh, "I can't help myself apparently."

"Mate," West whistles, "I wouldn't either. So what, you're…?"

"Vivian's bodyguard," I laugh, "Though I have more to do with Ray than I do with Vivian."

"Please tell me they have pillow fights in their underwear! *Please!*"

I narrow my eyes at him, "What is wrong with you? And why would I know that?"

He shrugs, "You've seen those movies, surely, you know those girl gangs where they sit around in their panties and talk about boys whilst they eat icecream."

"There is something wrong with you," I shake my head, "And if that does happen there's no way in hell I'd ever be privy to that."

"Well at least I can still fantasise about it," West shrugs, "So why'd you look so pissed?"

I wasn't pissed. I was frustrated and horny as hell. I had been since I had Ray pressed up against me back at the studio. I can still feel the warmth of her flowing over my skin like a caress. Shit, I jacked off in the shower to images of her bent over that very couch in the middle of the studio, moaning my name and clenching around my cock.

"Ray hates me," I sigh.

"So?" he shrugs, "It's not like you don't have a handful of women wanting in on your bed."

That was true. But I didn't want them.

"I don't know, man." I admit, taking a sip of my beer.

"You just need to find another woman," West shrugs.

Of course that would be his go to. The man had a revolving door of women coming in and out of his apartment here in LA. As a well-known agent he doesn't have a short supply of beautiful women coming into his office everyday and I'm pretty sure the man has never heard the word no before.

"Can I get you boys anything?"

"Well hi, Oli," West grins, showing teeth. His eyes hungrily take in the blonde at our table. I recognise her as one of Ray's friends.

"Weston," she replies coolly.

"No, we're good, thanks," I tell her.

"I'll take you," West tries.

She laughs abruptly, "Oh honey, you couldn't handle me."

I hide my laugh behind my hand.

"Oh, you'd be surprised at what I can handle." West continues.

"I've met your type," Oli throws back, "There's hardly anything to be surprised about." Her eyes drop to his crotch and she cocks a brow in a challenge.

Well maybe I was wrong and there are still women out there immune to whatever charms he has.

I'm thankful for the distraction, for a moment, whilst I watch the two of them bounce back and forth like a ping pong ball, Ray is pushed back a little in my mind.

"Why don't we head on out back and I'll show you."

"I'm a little old for show and tell," she pouts innocently, "But if that's all gentlemen, I have other patrons to serve."

West follows her with his eyes, lingering on her ass as she sways through the crowd and comes to a stop at a table of suits. Just like West, they eat her up like they're starved.

"I think I'm in love," he declares wistfully.

"Oh fuck off, man," I laugh, swatting him with the back of my hand.

"Nah you're right, ain't nobody got time for that shit."

I change the discussion to lighter topics but I still can't get *her* out of my damn head.

"Okay," West slurs drunkenly two hours later. He's on his seventh whiskey whilst I'm still nursing the same beer I came in with. It's warm and flat and completely unsatisfying but I'm drinking it anyway because once I finish I have to head home and I know damn well my dreams will once again be about Ray and I'm just not ready to torture myself yet. "But I don't understand why she doesn't want me." He's still talking about Oli who left an hour ago.

"Not everyone has to want you buddy."

"Yes but I've never been turned down before."

I roll my eyes and pull my phone from my jean pocket seeing I have several missed calls and a couple of texts.

Shit, I hadn't realised I'd left the thing on silent.

I unlock the phone and see they're missed calls from Ray and Vivian.

Oh shit.

I sit up straighter and open the text thread.

Where are you? I need to talk to you. That's from Ray.

I scroll down further.

Zach, I swear to God if you don't call me back! Again Ray.

"Give me a minute," I tell West, standing up from the table and heading outside where it's quieter. I dial Ray's number and wait a few seconds before she picks up.

"Oh finally," She says impatiently though her voice lacks the usual heat and if I'm not mistaken there's a shake in her tone.

"What is it?"

"Uh, can you come to Vivian's place?"

Is that *fear* in her voice?

"Ray, what the hell is going on?"

"Someone smashed up my car and we got another email."

I look at my watch, it's just gone eleven.

"They smashed up your car?"

"Yes, Zach." She sighs, "As in busted in my windscreen and slashed my tyres."

"What the fuck."

"My thoughts exactly."

"I'm on my way," I tell her and hang up.

I head back through to West and throw some money down on the table, way too much considering I only had a beer, but I need to get out of here so I don't really care.

"Where are you going?" He sits up straighter when he sees my face, "What happened?"

"Talk tomorrow," is all I reply and then I'm grabbing my helmet and heading back out to the bike. The journey over to Vivian's flies by in a blur and when I pull into the lot at the back of the apartment building, I have to pause to really take it in.

The car isn't just smashed up, it's been destroyed. All the windows are smashed, every tyre busted and dents mar every surface like someone has taken a baseball bat to it.

Ray is dancing from foot to foot, her thumbnail between her teeth. She looks fucking terrified and all I want to do is bring her into my body and shield her from all of this.

Nine

Ray

"What is going on between you two?" Vivian asks. She's sat on the couch with her knees tucked up under her chin. Our empty take out containers are scattered over her coffee table and I'm holding a fresh glass of wine. I can only have the one considering I'm driving but it's taken some of the tension from my body at least.

"Nothing is going on between us," I tell her.

"Well you looked real cosy back at the studio with him all pressed up into you like that."

I roll my eyes, of course she didn't see what happened prior to that. "That was nothing, he was just scaring off some photographer who got a little handsy."

Vivian bristles, "What do you mean, handsy?"

I sigh, "It was nothing. Don't worry about it."

Her eyes narrow, "Of course it matters, I swear you have the worst luck with men."

I laugh out loud, "Yeah, don't I know it! I told Harper I'm taking a man hiatus."

She grimaces, "Why would you do that?"

"Because hello, I attract those who genuinely believe a woman is only good for one thing."

She winces, "I don't think Zach would be like that." She wiggles her brows.

How were we even back on this topic!?

"Zach's an asshole."

"No he's not and you know it. There's some serious heat between you two and you can't deny that."

I roll my eyes. She wasn't wrong of course. The air crackled with the tension between us but I couldn't quite tell if that was just hostility or something more. Sexual maybe?

I sigh and take another sip of my wine, slouching down into the couch. I'm so glad I keep a bag of comfy clothes here for nights like this. I changed into my sweats and oversized hoodie the moment I stepped foot into her apartment, kicking off those damn heels that are trying to kill my feet.

I'm a shoe girl. Stereotypical of course but I love them, they're so pretty and make my legs look great so I'll bare the pain for the few hours I have to wear them.

I look down at the time on my phone and take the last mouthful of wine, "Right, I've got to go."

We had another busy day tomorrow and I still had a load of laundry to do when I got home.

"Okay, babe," Vivian chirps, "see you tomorrow."

I gather my things and pluck up my keys from the table by the door. I call my goodbyes over my shoulder and then take the elevator down. It isn't Thomas on the door tonight but a new guy. He's young, fresh faced but kind of sweet. He splutters every time we come into the building and if I didn't find it so amusing, I'd actually give him some pointers on how to talk to women. I head out the front doors and around the side of the building to where I'd parked my car this morning.

I'm not paying attention and it's only when my sneakers crunch over glass that I realise something's wrong.

I gasp when I look up.

My car!

Oh my fucking God!

My little mini has been battered to pieces. Every window is smashed in, every tyre slashed and the body has dents all over it.

The tablet pings with a new message and I knew the silence today was too good to be true. With tears in my eyes I pull it out and open the email app.

The longer you ignore our connection the worse it will get. Those closest to you will suffer.

Holy shit. The guy was going after Vivian's loved ones. Starting with me apparently.

I do the only thing I can think of, I call Zach.

It rings. And rings and rings.

"Hi you're through to Zach, I can't get to the phone right now, leave a message and I'll get back to you."

"Zach," my voice breaks and I bring my fingers up to my mouth to try and stifle the sob. "I need you. Call me back."

I fire off a text and then decide to have a good look at the car. The dents look like someone's taken a crowbar to the body, long, deep dents crumble the metal work. Both headlights have been caved in and I really have to wonder how whoever done this, managed to get away with it without the alarm going off or someone seeing.

I'm not able to stop the tears now. They're falling freely, wetting my cheeks, and blurring my vision. I try Zach again, but he doesn't answer.

I have a feeling he's ignoring me like he did today, so I send him a pissy message and then call Vivian to come down.

"Oh my God, Ray, I'm so sorry!" She cries, "This is my fault!"

A sob breaks through my throat, "No. This isn't. It's that creeps fault! We really need to contact the police."

She nods. "You're right."

I've just managed to stop the tears when Zach finally calls me back.

"Oh, finally," I shouldn't be rude considering the time of night I've called him at and he's not actually employed to deal with *my* issues but I guess this counts as Vivian's issue too.

"What is it?" He sounds tired. Oh shit, I hope I didn't wake him.

"Uh, can you come to Vivian's place?" I eye the car, fear clenching my stomach. This is getting bad.

"What the hell is going on?" He barks.

I fill him in and hang up with him promising to come to Vivian's immediately.

"Hey," Vivi wraps an arm around my shoulders, "Let's head back inside. Zach's coming yes?"

I nod, "I want to stay here."

Fresh tears have started to spill out. The car wasn't anything spectacular, but it was a brand new thing I bought with my own money. Money, I had worked hard to earn and now it's been taken away from me. Sure, insurance will help but it's not the point.

A motorbike pulls into the parking lot, the wheels screeching against the asphalt and my stomach clenches. The rider is dressed in a tight-fitting white t-shirt that hugs his muscles and a pair of distressed denim jeans with a helmet obscuring his face.

Surely that's not Zach, but no, that ink, whilst I only saw it once definitely belongs to him.

Zach throws his leg over the seat and unfolds himself to stand, pulling the helmet from his head. His hair is deliciously mused but his face is hard, expressionless.

His grey eyes scan over the car, his brows pulling down and then finds me, dancing from foot to foot with my thumb between my teeth.

He doesn't go to the car like I expect him to. No, instead, he crosses the space between us and pulls me into his chest, his thick arms folding around my body and holding me close.

The surprising comfort only brings on another round of tears and I really should be worried about getting mascara on his perfectly white tee. I take the comfort. My arms fold around his waist, my hands balling into fists on his back and bunching the material. I sob into his chest. I'm scared, something I don't like to admit, but being encased in his thick arms, his warmth caressing my skin provides a comfort I so desperately need. It's a comfort that settles into my bones, it's like home, like this is where I belong. And that nearly terrifies me more than my smashed car and the psychopath behind the emails.

"Shh," he murmurs, "I got you."

"That's my car," I hiccup.

"I know, sweetheart."

He holds me until I finally stop crying and then gently pushes me away, his eyes searching over my face. "Go inside, I'll be up in a minute." He nods to

Vivian and then she's curling me into her body and guiding me back into the building.

The young kid at the door says something but I hardly hear it. Back inside the apartment a warm cup of something is pressed into my hands but I feel numb to everything.

Distantly I hear the door open and close and then the couch dips next to me and Zach's unique scent wafts under my nose. I find myself leaning into him and he welcomes me, throwing one arm around my shoulders to tuck me into his body.

Here I feel safe. I feel protected.

"I've called the police," he tells me, "They're on the way."

I nod slowly.

"Did you see anything?" He asks, "Either of you?"

I shake my head whilst Vivian answers out loud, "No, we've been in the apartment all night. How did he do it without the alarm going off?"

I feel Zach shrug, "It's possible but he would have to know how to disconnect the battery to stop the alarm from sounding. I've spoken to the concierge, there's CCTV out in the lot so hopefully we'll have something from that. The cops will ask the other residents if they saw anything."

"Did you see the email?" Vivian asks.

"No."

I hated feeling helpless so taking a deep breath I pull myself away from Zach's heat and reach into my bag to pull out the tablet.

"I received it just after I saw the car." I tell him, my voice sounding way stronger than I felt.

His eyes narrow in on my face and then they look down at the email still open on the screen.

"So the guy started with you," Zach growls.

"I guess so, I haven't heard anything from Harper or Oli so I assume they're okay."

"I saw Oli at Franks," Zach informs, "She was fine."

"You were at Franks?" I ask.

He nods once.

"So I didn't wake you?"

"No," he shakes his head, rubbing a hand up my spine.

The buzzer shrills, making me jump and Zach's hand on me tightens, "It's alright. It's just the police."

I swallow and nod as Vivian buzzes them up. All I really want to do is curl in on myself. Even though the violence wasn't at me directly I can't help but feel completely vulnerable. How did he know that was *my* car? Was he watching when I found it? Is Vivian actually safe here?

Two uniformed officers step in but Zach never leaves my side. His arm stays firmly planted around my waist and whilst I'm not complaining at his closeness I find my brain isn't quite working the way it should. Like there's a lose wire and I'm short circuiting.

Is it normal for one person to completely steal your focus? And for it to happen so quick?

I didn't think he'd have this side to him, considering we'd only known each other a few days and those days had been filled with arguments, it shocks me that he's able to be this tender with me.

The officers ask me a bunch of questions, most of which I can't answer, they take statements and then they leave, promising to call when they have an update.

"We will need to make a statement about the stalking," Zach addresses Vivian, "I'll contact Hudson."

"I need to go home," I mumble.

I'm tired, worn out both mentally and physically and all I really want is my bed.

"I'll take you home." Zach tells me.

It doesn't register that he didn't come in the SUV, nothing really registers as we say goodbye to Vivian and he guides me to the elevator, his hand never leaving my lower back.

We walk into the parking lot, Zach turning me so I don't see my beaten up little mini and towards the flashy motorcycle parked with the helmet still perched on the seat.

He hands me the helmet and grins boyishly, "Hop on."

Ten

Zach

She stares at me like I just asked her to strip from her clothes and give me a private show, which if we were on better terms I might actually consider, but with the events of the night I don't think that's on the table.

"I can't get on that," a spark ignites in her eyes, one that's been missing since I turned up earlier.

"Course you can, it's like riding a bicycle, you put one leg over and hold on tight."

"That's a death machine!" She shrieks.

"Only if you don't know how to ride."

She eyes me and the bike warily but then swallows down that fear and takes the helmet from me, sliding it on over her head. I'd much prefer her to be in leathers as well but unfortunately I didn't bring any and I usually chose to go without. It's a rookie move because if I did come off the bike, my skin would not

70

be happy with the road rash that came with a fall, if I even survived it, but I'd never had a crash before and I was cocky.

She goes to throw one leg over but stumbles and I reach out quickly to steady her. She grips my forearm, her nails biting into my skin.

She huffs loudly and then using my arm as leverage, throws her long leg over the seat and settles in. I climb on in front of her, grab both her arms and place them around my waist.

"Hold on," I order. It's not soft or gentle, a command she will obey. Her hands take the material of my tee in her fists and the pressure of her against my arms settles right down to the bone. "Don't let go." I tell her more softly.

I feel her breasts pushing into my back and the heat between her thighs at the base of my spine.

Okay this was a bad idea.

Despite the events of the night blood rushes south with her so close. Have you ever tried to ride a bike with a hard on? Yeah – it's uncomfortable as shit.

I fidget subtly, hoping it'll rearrange the stiff erection in my jeans and turn the key, revving up the engine and feeling it rumble between my thighs.

Her arms tighten a fraction as I kick out the stand and then set off. If possible she settles in closer, squeezing a little too hard to make the ride safe.

"Ease up!" I yell over the wind.

She doesn't listen and I really have to focus not to swerve the bike off the road.

Somehow we make it back to her apartment building in one piece and I park it out front.

"I'll walk you up," I tell her, helping her take the helmet from her head.

"That was…" she breathes, her eyes wide.

"Scary?"

"Exhilarating," she giggles and shit that sound is like music.

I swallow down the feeling, "Maybe I'll take you for another ride one day."

I choke on my tongue when I play the words back in my head.

If she takes the words wrong she doesn't show it, just hands me back the helmet and turns to walk into her apartment building. I follow her, my fingers itching to reach out and touch her. Having her close earlier, tucked into my side where I could keep her safe felt more right than it had any right to be. I know she only allowed it because she felt vulnerable but there was something about her, something that resonated inside of me that told me she was right where she belonged.

"You don't have to walk me all the way up," she says as she stops in front of the elevator and presses the button.

"It's okay." I tell her.

Her smile is small and whilst we wait she wraps her arms around herself, staring directly ahead at the metal doors in front of her.

God. This was awkward.

I dig my hands into the pockets of my jeans and tip my chin back, stifling my sigh as I stare at the white ceiling in the foyer of the building. There's no concierge here and as we step into the elevator there's no code to get you up to the floors above, just a number of buttons with apartment numbers listed next to them.

She hits the button for her floor and curls into herself in the corner of the cart.

"I'm sorry about your car," I break the silence.

This must be the longest elevator ride in history. Being trapped in a small metal box with this woman was dangerous.

It was temptation reincarnated, lust and greed and gluttony all mixed into one to create a sin so deadly it's about to eat me alive.

"Thank you." She answers, "It's a bit shit but at least I have insurance."

"We'll find the guy," and as I say it, I vow to make the words true. If not for Vivian, because she was a good girl after all but for Ray. I doubt this whole thing has been easy on her, having to see the emails as they come in, to read the threats and violence first-hand.

The elevator dings as it reaches her floor and the doors slowly slide open. She steps out and turns left in the hall, heading down towards a plain white door at the end.

She pulls her keys from her purse and then turns to me.

"This is me."

"Are you okay?" I ask, "After everything tonight?"

She shrugs, "I guess. Just a bit of a shock I suppose, it's a little scary knowing he knows stuff about me, like the car I drive. It makes sense, I mean he's trying to get close to Vivian, he's going to have to find out stuff about us, me and the girls."

I nod. "I've dealt with this before," I tell her, "I'm sure it won't get much worse than this."

She laughs without humour, "Well I hope so."

A long silence stretches between us.

"Anyway, thank you. Good night."

Ah fuck it!

"Ray, wait," I step into her space, tip her chin back and plant my lips on hers.

She stiffens under me and it's a moment before she melts right into me. My hands cup either side of her face, fingers sliding into her hair, feeling the tresses twirling around the tips. My tongue demands entry and she obliges, opening her mouth to let me inside.

Her hands sit on my waist, her fingers digging in a little as I deepen the kiss, tipping her chin back further as I demand more.

Shit she tastes good. So fucking good.

My tongue tangles with hers and without thinking I press her back into the door. Her back makes a thud with the force of it but she doesn't let up on my mouth, no she tugs me closer until my body is flush with hers.

A delicious little moan escapes her throat and I swallow that shit down like it's sustenance.

I hear locks disengaging but it doesn't quite register until the door flies open behind her back and she tumbles backwards, falling right out of my arms and landing on her backside in the threshold of the door. I almost follow her if I hadn't managed to grip the door frame to stop myself from crushing her with my weight.

"Oof!" She exhales.

"What the fuck is going on?" Her little red headed friend exclaims. Her eyes move from her friend on the floor to me and those green eyes widen in shock, "Holy shit!"

Ray opens her mouth like she wants to say something but then closes it, shaking her head as if to clear it from a daze. I know the feeling. My head is a swirling mess of fog right now and all I can think about is stripping her from those clothes shielding her body from me.

I reach forward and grip her hand, tugging her up off

the floor.

"You okay?"

She closes her eyes, "Fine, thank you."

Her conservative reply catches me off guard and I bring my hand back from her. "Right, well. You ladies have a good night."

With that I get the fuck out of there.

"Zach, wait!" Ray shouts after me.

"I'll see you tomorrow!" I call back, punching the button for the elevator more times than really necessary.

I step in and the metal doors slide closed behind me and I take my first breath since that kiss.

That kiss.

I'm a man that's been with his fair share of women over the years, sure I wasn't proud of it but it is what it is, but I've never had a kiss like that. That was…that was, I don't even have words to describe.

That was like the sun rising in the morning and the waves crashing on the shore. That was the kiss to end all kisses and I have no idea how to go on without having another one.

I suck in a lungful of clean air when I step back outside and then slip my helmet over my head, throwing my leg over the seat. I need more air. I need more time to think about the shit that went down tonight.

That was the wrong time to kiss her. Completely the wrong time.

Instead of heading back to the condo I drive the coastal roads through the city, stopping a few times to listen to the water. The moon sits fat and round in the midnight sky, a few stars peeking through the light pollution that stifles their shine. The engine of my bike purrs in the silence of the night, echoing down the empty alleys and bouncing off darkened office buildings. I pass a few late night party goers but my head, it can't clear itself of Ray.

Eventually it gets so late that my eyes start to get heavy and I have to go home to the call of my bed. I park the bike in the underground garage and make my way up to the condo, scrubbing my hand through my hair on my way and tugging on the ends a little.

I strip out of my clothes, the lingering scent of Ray hits my nose as I pull my tee over my head. Citrusy and sweet and my mouth waters, remembering the way her tongue pressed into mine, demanding and needy and the way her hands held me close as if even an inch between us wouldn't do.

My skin remembers the way her breasts felt pressed up against my back and then my chest and how her needy hands roamed over my body, searching and exploring.

Just how far would that have gone in that quiet hallway if her friend hadn't interrupted. With the way my cock reacts to her, it would have tried for more, so much more, taking and taking again anything she would be willing to give.

I stare up at my darkened ceiling.

Shit just got real.

Eleven

Ray

"What the hell did I just witness?" Harper exclaims when I numbly make my way into the apartment and collapse down on to the couch.

"Zach kissing me," I answer honestly.

"Well I got that much," she hisses, "But why!?"

Why? I have no idea.

He kissed me and I didn't stop him. I didn't want to stop him either. The way his lips felt on mine was too good, too perfect to even think about denying them. I still feel his phantom presence against me, his hard muscles on my chest, his hands cupping my face.

He was gentle and yet demanding, soft but fierce in his need for the kiss.

I shouldn't have let him kiss me. I really shouldn't have. There's just some lines that shouldn't be crossed. I've had a shitty night, I'm vulnerable and a little freaked by the events but that kiss felt real.

"I don't know," I answer Harper's question, "I really don't know."

"I thought you disliked each other."

"We do."

"Yeah, it looks real tense between the two of you. Shit Ray, it looked like you were about rip each others clothes off."

To be honest, that probably would have happened had she not opened the door. I should feel embarrassed that I literally fell on my ass but all I feel is heat and not the embarrassed kind. No this heat sat much lower. God I was so fucking turned on, just from that kiss that I'm actually worried for my sexual health. No man has ever made me this hot without even so much as trying.

"Vivian called," Harper says, "I heard about your car. I'm so sorry, Raynie."

I swallow, pushing all thoughts of Zach from my head. There're much more important things to think about other than Zach fucking Wyatt.

"Yeah," I say, "It's a bit shit."

"A bit shit?" Harper scoffs, "It's terrible!"

"Yeah, thanks Harp, I don't need the reminder."

"Sorry," She winces.

I sigh, "Sorry, I didn't mean to snap."

She settles down on the couch besides me, "It's okay, you've had a crazy night."

I nod, "I'm going to head to bed. I'll see you in the morning."

After stripping down to just a pair of panties and a tank top I climb under the sheets and proceed to stare up at the darkened ceiling. I reach over to my phone and pull up my texts to Zach.

Thank you I type and then delete. *What was that kiss?*

I delete that too. Fuck, what do I say? Do I say anything at all?

Goodnight. Before I can talk myself out of it, I hit the send button and then switch my phone off. I don't want to just ignore him, not after tonight but after that kiss, has things changed between us? Are we no longer enemies? Are we friends?

Shit.

I scrub my hands over my eyes and toss myself onto my side, facing the window and staring out at the swollen moon hanging over the ocean. My body is burning too hot, my muscles wound tight.

That kiss has ignited something inside me, something furious and demanding and it has more to do with Zach than I care to admit.

—

I slide my feet into my favourite pair of burgundy heels with the little peep toes and smooth my hands down the front of my black dress. It has a tight bodice with little capped sleeves and a flowing skirt that teases my frame but doesn't quite give it away.

I've left my hair down today and curled the ends so they bounce against the tops of my breasts and my make-up is light with only a tinted gloss over my lips.

With a nod at myself in the mirror I head out to the kitchen. Harper is already in the kitchen which is shocking considering she's never up before I am and she's making coffee. I smell the hearty aroma of the miracle juice and groan, my caffeine fix in need of replenishment.

She hands me over my travel mug that reads *Too Glam to give a Damn* and I take a sip, closing my eyes.

Yes, I have a serious caffeine addiction, no I'm not willing to stop.

"You look nice," Harper comments, sipping at her own coffee, "I wonder why that is."

"I always look nice," I throw back with a smirk.

She clucks her tongue, "Sure you do but I mean, that dress, that's the big guns, is someone out to impress by any chance?"

"No, of course not," I lie. Maybe I am little.

"Anyway, I've got to go!"

"Ray, what about–"

I go to reach into the bowl where I usually keep my keys and come up empty handed. How had I forgotten about the car already? My arm drops to my side and I just stare at the empty space. What the hell am I going to do now?

"Here," Ray snatches up her own keys, "I'll drive you over to Vivi's before going to the store. Give me a minute to get dressed!"

I nod slowly, sucking my bottom lip into my mouth only to be rewarded with the sticky taste of my lip-gloss. It smells like cherry but let me tell you, it does not taste like it at all.

I chase away the taste with my coffee and perch on the edge of the arm on the couch. I pull my phone from the front pocket of my purse and switch it on for the first time since I text Zach last night.

One message pops up and then a second message, both from him.

Goodnight, sweetheart. He sent that only seconds after I sent the first one. The second message is from this morning.

I'll pick you up. Be ready at 8.30.

I look at the clock. It's only eight so I text back and tell him it's fine and that I'll meet him at Vivian's and then lock the phone and put it back in my bag.

Little bubbles of nerves have started to pop in my stomach. Are things going to be different between us now? Did he regret kissing me? Did I?

There's so much to do, I need to get hold of the insurance people and speak to the cops again and I can barely think straight.

Harper and I make our way downstairs and into the parking lot. The sun is already burning hot, the sky a perfect cloudless blue. The sounds of horns honking and tyres screeching fills my ears. Everything is normal.

But I don't feel normal.

I'm quiet on the way over to Vivian's place and I'm here before Zach is. I say my goodbyes to Harper where she's dropped me in front of the building.

Part of me wants to detour around the back to see if last night actually happened. Would my car still be there or would it have been collected by now?

Instead of torturing myself, I head into the lobby, smiling at Thomas behind the desk.

"Miss Stone," Thomas gives me a sympathetic smile, "I heard about the car. I'm so sorry. That's never happened here before."

I shrug, "The cops are looking into it."

"Yes well, where I can help I will."

"Thanks Thomas, have a good day."

I punch my code into the elevator and head up to Vivian's apartment. She's ready to go when she opens the door. "Where's Zach?" She looks over my shoulder.

"On his way I guess," I tell her, "Harper dropped me off."

"They collected your car this morning," Vivian

informs me and answers my own question. "Hudson is furious."

"Hardly surprising," I shrug, "That man is fiercely protective over you."

"It's not me he's worried about, Ray, it's you."

"I'll be fine. We just need to figure this guy out and getting the cops involved will hopefully help. Cars are replaceable."

"You're being very understanding about this," Vivian frowns, "I'd be spitting feathers if it were me."

I think about the events of last night. Was I angry? I'm not sure. I was shocked. A little scared but all that disappeared when Zach arrived. It wasn't when he kissed me, no it was when he stormed across the parking lot and pulled me into his arms. It was when he told me he had me. At that point, despite our mutual *dislike* – if that's even what you can call it now – of each other, I realised he's the protector, the wall between us and them.

The force to be reckoned with.

Twelve

Zach

Ray avoids me for the rest of the week. If there's even a slight chance that we're going to be left alone together she hightails it out of there, making up excuses left and right.

At first it was amusing. Now it's just pissing me off.

It's Friday morning and Vivian is sat in a radio station recording an interview with the resident DJ and Ray is nowhere to be found. I stand with my arms folded across my chest trying to think of a way to get her with me so we can talk.

I pull my phone from the inside pocket of my suit jacket and dial her number. It rings twice before she presses the decline button.

She fucking declined my call.

I try again but the same thing happens.

You can't ignore me forever. I type out and send. It's read immediately but no response comes.

Jesus Christ that woman was stubborn.

RAY!

Nothing.

"How long is left on the interview mate?" I ask one of the guys sat on this side of the glass with me.

"Twenty minutes or so."

"Alright, I'm going to get coffee."

He nods and I leave, trying my damnedest not to slam my way through the building.

I was frustrated. Frustrated and so goddamn confused that my patience has really worn thin.

I didn't even know what the fuck I wanted but what I did know, was that I wanted her to talk to me. Just fucking talk.

It doesn't even have to be about the kiss, hell her car was busted up, she really needs to talk about it or something. Vivian has told me she's just brushed it under the carpet but was worried after the last email came in.

You went to the cops. That was a mistake. That's all it said but all we've had since is radio silence. It's probably scared the guy off. He deserved to pay for what he'd done but I wouldn't be complaining if he just upped and disappeared. If I ever got my hands on him he'd definitely start to regret his choices. Fuckers like that deserved all the shit. Scaring women was despicable. Threatening them was even worse.

I take the steps down to the on-site cafeteria two at a time. Ray's probably downing copious amounts of coffee like she did on the daily. I have no idea how she's not just shaking all the time with the amount of caffeine flowing through her veins. A few people step out of my way as I close the distance between me and the cafeteria, probably sensing my irritation and wanting to avoid a stand off.

The doors rattle as I push them open and she's exactly where I thought she would be.

She sits at one of the little round tables near the wall of windows. Her phone is pressed to her ear and a mug of coffee is clutched in her palm.

My legs eat up the space between us and then I'm staring down at her.

Her eyes drag up my body and then widen when she finally finds my face.

"A word." Is all I say.

"Yes, Oli, I've gotta go," she says on the phone.

My nostrils flare as her mouth-watering scent drifts past my nose and my fingers twitch with the need to reach out and tuck a strand of hair behind her ear that's fallen from her ponytail. "Yes, I'll see you tonight."

Ah that's right. Girls night out. And I'm on shift seeing as Vivian needs a bodyguard. Truthfully, I could have gotten one of the stand in guys to do it, but Ray will be out and I've seen her drunk before. The idea that she'll be in a middle of a club, no doubt in a dress that'll make her look like a goddess with guys lusting after her made my stomach clench with nausea.

I'm possessive when I have no right to be. I'll never tell her that though.

"Can I help you?" Her tone is dismissive and she looks back down at the pad resting on the table.

"What the hell is your problem?" I growl, low enough so it doesn't draw attention to the others in the room.

"Excuse me?" She bristles. I scoff, as if she's actually offended.

"You're avoiding me. Why?"

"I am not," she defends, balling her little hands into

fists, "I'm just very busy."

I place my palm over her tablet, "Care to look at me when we're talking?"

Her eyes bounce from the tablet to my face and the blues are alive with fire. Yes. There it is. The fire in her I've come to enjoy.

"We have nothing to talk about."

"What about the other night?"

Her shoulders tense. So that's why she's avoiding me. Because I kissed her. I don't regret it. Not one single bit. I'd do it again too. I'd probably do it now if I weren't so afraid she'd castrate me if I tried.

"Not here," I tell her and then stride back to the door. She'll follow. Her curiosity will eat at her until her body is moving without her permission. When I hear the clip of her heels behind me a satisfied smirk tugs on my lips. I saw a storage closet down here somewhere.

When I find it, I push open the door and step inside, leaving the light off.

"Zach?" Ray's tentative voice is small as she steps in through the door.

I grip her around the wrist and gently tug her into the room, closing the door behind her.

The room is small and I can feel her body almost touching mine, the air around us still. I hear the hitch in her breath.

"Why are you avoiding me, sweetheart?" I say softly, dipping my head until I can feel her hair tickling my chin.

"I'm not," she breathes, "Zach, why are we in a closet?"

It's too dark in here to be able to see her face but I can almost hear the blood rushing to her cheeks.

"Why not?"

"Well because there's hardly any room to breathe in here let alone have this conversation."

"What conversation would that be?" I press.

"God, you're insufferable," She huffs, exasperated, "The kiss."

I chuckle lightly, "Oh sweetheart, I actually only wanted to ask how you're feeling but if you insist."

Suddenly she shoves me, she puts all her weight into it too, but I barely move.

"Why do you have to be such an ass!"

I step into her space, pressing my chest into hers, "Why do you have to be so stubborn?" I retort.

"I'm not stubborn," She crosses her arms, forcing me back a little.

"No?"

"No."

"You are a little."

"No, Zach I'm not. You just don't know when to take a hike."

"Is that right?" I lean in, my lips millimetres away from her ear, "You telling me you haven't thought about that kiss? About how I felt pressed into your bod?. You telling me you didn't fall asleep wondering what it would feel like to have my mouth on other parts?"

"I – I didn't think about it," she stammers though the lie falls short. I hear it for what it is.

"I think you did," I tell her, "You're thinking about it now too. You want me to kiss you again, don't you?"

Her breath fans my face, "We can't."

"Just say the word, Ray," *Please*, "Just say it."

The air pulses around us, pressing against my heated skin. I feather my fingers up her bare arm, revelling in the feel of her beneath my hands. I can only imagine what she'd be like under me, her head thrown back in pleasure.

She wants to be rocked. I'd make sure she couldn't even remember her own name.

"Zach," It's a plea.

I follow the curve of her shoulder until I can grip the back of her neck, tilting her chin up.

I run the tip of my nose down the slant of hers, my lips barely whispering against hers.

"If you won't say it," it's pure torture but I step back from her. Everything in me is screaming to claim her. Make her mine but she won't admit that she wants me.

I'm bad news.

"You're such an ass," she seethes.

"So you keep saying, sweetheart," I'm glad I'm able to mask the frustration in my voice. The huskiness, yeah that's not so easy to hide. My reaction to her is evident in the tent I'm currently sporting in my pants.

I open the door and the cool air of the hall hits me.

"Pig!" She yells after me.

"Come find me when you're ready to admit you want me." I call back.

"That'll be never!" Her long legs closes the gap between us and she falls into step as I make my way back up to the studio.

I shrug like it's not a big deal, "I guess you'll never know what it's like to be *rocked* then."

A furious blush flushes through her cheeks and she opens her mouth and then closes it, unable to throw anything back.

I leave her standing in the hall. Her little body is filled with a rage aimed directly at me, her hands balled into fists and blues alive with fire. It'll be fun to work it out of her.

Preferably in the bedroom.

Rock Me

Naked.
Very, very naked.

Thirteen

Ray

I throw back the wine in my glass. "No, he's an ass and all I want to do is," I mimic my hands wrapping around someone's throat, "strangle him."

"Naked?" Oli giggles from her spot on the couch.

"No!" I hiss, going back to search through my hall closet for the other black heel I was planning on wearing tonight. My ass is probably on show but I'm too pissed off to care right now.

Vivian skips past me and swats my backside with the back of her hand, prancing out of the way when I try to swat her back.

"Oh she definitely wants to get naked with him," Vivian declares.

"Who's getting naked?" Harper saunters from her room.

"Ugh!" I grumble. Three against one is totally not

fair.

"Zach and Ray."

"No we're not!" I stamp my foot and then I spot the heel I've been looking for tucked beneath a box at the bottom of the closest. I yank it out and slam the closet door, heading back to top up my wine glass.

"I don't know what went down today," Vivian continues, "But I swear you could cut the tension between them with a knife."

"If you're all finished, how about we actually do some drinking instead of making up weird sexual fantasies about me and Vivian's bodyguard."

"It'll only be fantasy for so long," Oli singsongs.

I roll my eyes and pull tequila from the top shelf. I need it.

"Why are you so against anything happening between you and Zach anyway?" Harper asks, joining the girls in the living room. She looks cute in a tight pair of faux leather trousers and a little red crop top, a little pair of heeled boots on her feet.

Thankfully she hasn't divulged that she caught us kissing only a few days ago. We're all close friends here but Harper and I are more like sisters. She knows when to keep a secret.

I haven't told any of the girls about what happened back at the radio station. About how Zach cornered me in a tiny closet under the ruse of 'checking on me' when really, all he wanted to do was tease me. I should have known.

He's so sure of himself. So sure I want him. And I might. I mean the man is a god to look at, all wrapped up in tightly muscled, heavily tattooed body. But just because he's attractive doesn't mean he gets to have the complex to go with it. Arrogance isn't attractive.

Okay, it is a little on him, but I have more respect for myself than to drop to my knees in front of him. I can control myself.

It doesn't matter that I haven't been able to shake the desire he lit in me, it doesn't matter that my muscles literally ache for him. I *can* and I *will* control myself.

If I just keep repeating that then we'll all be fine.

Zach and I. That would disastrous.

Bad. News.

I pour out four shots and hand them to the girls, "To us." I toast, "To the few days of silence we've had," I pointedly look at Vivian, "To being fierce," I look to Oli, "To being kind," Harper, "And to being strong, independent women."

"Who don't need no man," They all call back.

We throw the shots back just as the buzzer for the apartment sounds. That'll be Zach.

I've got this. I can do this.

Harper skips to the door and lets him up and I have a few minutes before he gets here to compose myself. I take stock of myself. Cute little black dress, it sits high on the thigh but the neckline wraps around my throat with a clasp. My hair is pulled into a voluminous ponytail and I've gone for a dramatic smoky eye look with deep burgundy lips.

Tonight's about letting loose a little, it's no secret that I've been wound so tight it'll only be a matter of time before I snap. What tonight isn't about is Zach and his arrogant, cocky ways even if I can't escape him.

"Ladies," Zach's deep rumble of a voice shoots right through me, rattling my bones.

"I swear he gets better looking every time I see him," Harper hisses in my ear.

I narrow my eyes at her and then shake my head, "Keep your panties on."

She cocks a brow, "I could say the same to you."

I step into the living room. I can look at him and not be floored. I mean he's only a man, it's not like his mere presence will drop my panties.

Oh shit.

He's in suit pants, tight suit pants that mould to his thighs and his white shirt is tucked into the belt. There's no suit jacket tonight and he's rolled the sleeves up to his elbows, showing off his tanned and tattooed, muscular forearms. The top few buttons are un-popped and he's had a shave, not clean, just enough that there's a shadow across his jaw. His grey eyes meet mine and I swear they flare brighter when he looks at me. His eyes drag down my body and one of his brows cocks as he scrubs a hand across his mouth.

What is it about that move that's so god damned sexy?

Steeling myself against him, I jerk my chin out, square my shoulders and strut to the door. I will prove to him that he does not affect me.

"Ray," he murmurs quietly as I pass, "You look beautiful."

And I trip.

I was not expecting that.

He's quick to reach out and steady me, lacing one hand around my middle to stop me from face planting the hard floor. His fingers dig into my waist but then he removes them quickly, leaving only heat in their wake.

So much for not affecting me. Shit.

"Thanks," I flatten out non-existent creases in my dress and pick up my clutch, swallowing down the golf ball sized lump in my throat. When I turn back to the girls they're all giving me knowing smiles, eyes bouncing between me and Zach who is still looking at me.

"Are we ready?" I say nervously, "let's go."

I make sure I'm way ahead of them as I get to the elevator and punch the button, the heel of my shoe tapping impatiently.

"I get tingles just looking at you two," Oli sidles up next to me.

"Mmm," the girls agree.

"There's something wrong with you," I whisper hiss, "All of you."

I press myself into the furthest corner from Zach when we get in the elevator but he's everywhere. In my head, in my senses, I can't fucking escape.

—

We're whizzed to the front of the line, ushered through the door and up the stairs, straight to the roped off VIP area of the club downtown. The club is tinged in pink and purple lights, music thumps loudly through the speakers but at least we don't have to fight to get a table. We follow the suit wearing server to a booth at the edges of a dancefloor which is already packed with people grinding to the music. A bottle of champagne sits in a bucket of ice in the middle of the table and as we're being seated, a bottle of grey goose is bought to the us as well as another bucket of mixers.

"See I knew there was a reason we were friends with you," Oli laughs, popping the cork on the champagne.

"Bitch," Vivi chuckles lightly, taking the offered flute. Zach stands just off to the side, far enough away that we can talk without him hearing but close enough should something go wrong.

We were all still getting used to how Vivian's popularity had grown over the past few months and even now, a group a few tables down from us are whispering and throwing looks at our table. With the video for Nate's new song soon to be released she was only going to grow more.

She was still humble though. I honestly believe she could be the most famous woman in the world and she'd still walk round in her bunny slippers and come to brunch on Sundays. The fame doesn't bother her, even with this whole stalker situation, she's graceful and kind.

We haven't heard a whisper from the guy all week. The cops are still looking into it and the insurance is dealing with my car. Maybe Zach's right and the idea of the authorities being involved has scared the guy off.

I take the flute of champagne from Oli and take a sip, already feeling slightly buzzed from the half bottle of wine I'd devoured before leaving the apartment. I feel the tension from the past week easing from my shoulders and I sigh contentedly. Maybe the worst of it was over. Hudson would be happy with that. He's been battling the press since it was leaked about the car situation. There's a lot of speculation but he's managed to keep most of it at bay.

With that in mind, I make a vow to enjoy myself tonight.

Fourteen

Zach

Dresses like that need to be illegal.

She looks fucking stunning.

"Zach!" I hear my name hollered from behind me and reluctantly, I drag my gaze away from the girls dancing on the floor to see West pushing his way through the crowd. Hudson is behind him and another guy I haven't met.

"What the fuck are you doing here?" I meet his hand, slapping my palm into his.

"Well you did say you were escorting the girls out tonight, I couldn't resist," he grins. He spots the four of them dancing, his pupils dilating as he takes them in. I swear to god if he's looking at Ray, I'll punch him in the throat.

I greet Hudson next, "I didn't know you knew each other."

"We don't," Hudson grumbles, "he does," he jerks

his head to the large guy to his side, "This is Declan, a buddy of mine. He's worked with Vivian a lot and apparently these two are friends."

"Fuck that girl is on fire," West yells. I follow his gaze to where Oli is dropping real low to the floor. I turn back to Hudson and his friend, my eyes narrowing in on the newcomer. He's watching Vivian intently, not in an admiring way. There's something seedy about him. I make a note to keep an eye on him.

"I'm sure the girls will be happy to see you," I tell Hudson.

"Actually, I wanted to have a word with you," Hudson tells me. "Get us some drinks?" He asks Declan.

The big guy wonders off, beelining to the girls but not stopping. Instead he turns his head to watch Vivian dancing with Ray, barely taking an eye off her as he orders drinks.

"What's up?"

"What's going on between you and Ray?" He gets right to it.

"Me and Ray?" I laugh, "Nothing." *Yet*.

"You sure about that?"

"Pretty sure, mate."

"I feel like an absolute dick right now," Hudson grumbles to himself, "Ray's like a little sister to me. She means a lot and whilst threatening you will likely end badly for me, I'm going to anyway. Hurt her and I'll hurt you."

I can't help it. I laugh. Out loud.

It stops abruptly when I see the very serious look on his face. "Oh you're serious."

"Yes, Zach, I'm serious."

"You don't have to worry, man," I slap a hand on his

shoulder, "There's nothing going on anyway."

His eyes narrow but lets it go and goes to the girls, hugging Vivian and Ray first before moving to the other two. That Declan dude is hanging at the edges.

"Who is that guy?" I ask West, jerking my chin to the guy.

"Who Declan?"

I nod once.

"He owns a studio we use for shoots a lot," West tells me, "He's a good guy."

He wasn't a good guy. Call it intuition but there was something about him that had my hackles raising.

I lean against the back of the booth seats and cross my arms over my chest, eyes landing on Ray as she and Harper dance. The hem of her dress is slipping up her thigh and it's already dangerously short. Her long ponytail flicks back and forth but she's happy, the happiest I've seen since I met her. She wiggles her hips and rolls her shoulders to the music. They've devoured a bottle of champagne and half of the vodka that was left on their table.

Drunk Ray was cute.

She was talkative and easy. She'd already spoke to me a few times tonight, nothing important, more word vomit than anything else.

"You've got it so bad," West laughs, "Shit, does that mean I need a new wing man?"

"I've never been your wingman," I tell him, ignoring the first comment.

Declan has moved into the circle, he's talking to Vivian, his body only a few inches from hers and by the look on Hudson's face he's not enjoying it one bit.

Suddenly the music changes to an old club classic and the crowd on the dance floor pulses. It happens in slow motion, I swear. Someone shoves into the girls and then they disappear into the folds of the crowd.

"Shit," I hiss. West follows my line of vision and follows me as I push through the crowd. Shoving bodies out the way as I force myself through the girls. West is behind me. Ray has got some guy by the collar of his shirt, her face a mask of fury. Vivian is behind Hudson's body and Oli and Harper have been shoved behind Declan. What the fuck is going on?

I grab the guy Ray is holding by the neck of his shirt, yanking him back. He holds his hands up in surrender and quickly scurries away. Someone shoves into my back, pushing me forward into Ray.

I grab her around the waist to stop her from tumbling over and plant my feet, balancing myself.

I fucking hate night clubs.

"What the hell happened?" I growl at her. Shit. This isn't her fault.

She curls her hands into my shirt and shakes her head, looking behind her to the girls. "I don't know."

West has moved in on Oli and is talking in her ear, probably trying to find out what happened too. I jerk my head at Hudson, motioning him to get Vivian back to the table. There's too many people out here to be able to keep an eye on them all so they'll have to sit this dance out. Hudson nods once and guides Vivian back to the table whilst I grip Ray to my side and push my way back out of the crowd. She doesn't fight me, just holds on tight.

I use my elbows to get people to move out of my way and then we're free of the crowd.

"The fucker stood on my foot," Ray hisses, dropping down into the booth and lifting said foot onto the seat, kicking off the heel in the process.

It's already bruising over the top, near her toes which

are painted pink – I really shouldn't notice this shit.

"Here, let me see," I crouch, taking her foot from her hand.

I really shouldn't be doing this either.

My thumb strokes over the sore spot. I didn't need to see it or touch it, there's nothing wrong with it but any excuse to touch her.

Harper and Oli drop down on the other side of the table, followed by the guys and I snatch my hands away, "You're fine."

She nods. "Thanks."

"What the fuck happened?" Oli grumbles, lifting her glass to her lips.

"Just a couple of guys getting happy on the dancefloor," Hudson advises, "Idiots."

I grumble my agreement and then step back, going back to my position as watchman.

Dread begins to prickle at my senses and my eyes scan the club. Something isn't quite right. I can't focus on it for too long though, not when Ray stands from the table and starts to walk away.

I chase after her, "Where are you going?"

She cocks a brow, "Bathroom."

I eye the distance to the bathroom and then let her go seeing as I don't really have much choice.

When ten minutes pass and she still hasn't returned, that sense of dread really starts to pound in my head. I look over to Hudson who's talking quite intimately with Vivian but manage to snag his attention.

"Watch them," I mouth. He frowns but nods his head and I go off in search for my girl.

My girl.

Ha. Well shit.

I round the corner that will take me to the bathrooms but what I see has my blood running cold. And then really fucking hot and as my vision sees red, I charge.

Fifteen

Ray

I roll my eyes as I step away from Zach and head towards the bathrooms on the other side of the club. My foot was throbbing, and these heels really weren't helping but above all else, I really had to pee! With the amount alcohol I've consumed the dam is about to burst.

I wait patiently in the small queue for the ladies and once I'm in and done I step up to the sinks and wash my hands, checking over my face to make sure my make-up is still in place.

Before leaving I touch up my lipstick and then step out into the hall.

I'm just making my way back to the main club when a body steps in front of me.

"Sorry excuse me," I make a step to go round but the body follows me.

"Ray," I recognise the voice and it has me dragging

my gaze up.

My breath lodges in my throat when I see Sam staring down at me.

I look behind me and then in front, but I can't see past his body in front of me.

"Please move," I'm not even going to try to be polite.

"Maybe we got off on the wrong foot," He tries.

"You touched me inappropriately," I snap, "So yeah, I'd say so."

"I'd really like to take you out," he says, stepping into my body. I step back, trying to widen the gap between our bodies. Chills run over my skin at the way he's looking at me. It's not admirable, it's possessive and controlling.

"I don't think so," I tell him.

"Oh come on, Ray," Sam runs a finger up my arm, "We'd be so good together."

"I'd really like to leave," I tamper down the shake in my voice. I don't like feeling vulnerable.

Suddenly his hand clamps around my arm and he pushes me back. My back thuds against the wall hard, the back of my skull bouncing off the plaster.

"When will you realise that I'd be good for you," he growls menacingly. This wasn't a guy used to being turned down, that's for sure.

"Get off me!" I hiss.

"Hey, is everything okay here?" A small female voice says from the side of us.

"Fine," Sam barks at her.

The girl gets the fuck outta of there. I can't say I blame her.

"Get off me," I repeat, wincing at the pain his fingers are causing on my arm. He's holding tight enough to bruise.

He leans in close and I turn my head, squeezing my eyes closed. He inhales deeply and then suddenly he's gone.

Holy shit.

I sag down the wall but the sounds of grunts has my eyes springing open.

Oh. My. God.

"Zach!" I yell. His fist flies, landing a clean blow to the side of Sam's face.

He doesn't stop at one, no, he lands another two in before I come to my senses. I rush over, grab Zach's shoulders and tug.

I groan as I try to pull him off but it's like moving a fucking tank. His face is mask of fury and violence, eyes so dark I hardly recognise him.

"Zach," I screech.

Terror grips my stomach. Holy shit, he was going to kill the guy.

As if my voice is a balm his fist stops halfway to Sam's face. My eyes dart to him to survey the damage. A bloody nose, a split eyebrow but nothing an ice pack won't sort out.

"Ray," he whispers, his eyes closing.

"Yeah, it's me," I pull him and this time he lets me, coming up from where he's crouched over Sam.

"He touched you," it's not a question.

"I'm fine," I tell him. "I'm fine."

His dark melted silver eyes search my face as if he has to make sure I'm not lying.

I nod, "I'm okay."

My heart might just melt a little at the way he's looking at me right now. He looks so tortured I can't help myself. I step up to him, wrap my arms around his middle and rest my head against his chest. His heart is pounding furiously inside his chest, so hard I worry it's about to crack a rib. He doesn't miss a beat, his arms envelope me and then he's guiding us out of the hall, back towards the crowd of the club.

We don't head back to the table like I expect, no he pulls me down the side and into a vacant booth, pushing me down into the seat that seems to be shrouded in shadow like a curtain, hiding us away from the rest of the club.

"Let me see," he says, voice low, "Let me make sure you're okay."

"Zach," I cup his face, bringing his eyes level with mine, "I'm fine. He didn't hurt me."

His eyes run over my body, over my chest, torso and legs and then arms. His eyes snag at the top of my left arm. The same arm Sam had gripped only a few moments ago.

"He hurt you," He growls.

"No, I'm fine."

His nostrils flare, "Say something, anything, otherwise I'm going to go back there and I'm going to do something that won't let me walk out of here."

I search my brain, trying to find something to say, "What's your favourite colour?"

"What?"

"Your favourite colour, what is it?"

His eyes bounce between mine, his brows puckering, "Blue."

"Your favourite band?"

"I don't have one."

"What about family? You said you had a brother?"

"Yes."

"Zach, work with me here," I beg, "take your mind off of it."

"Kiss me."

My head snaps back, "What?"

"Kiss me." He repeats.

"I – I don't think that's a good idea."

"Kiss me Ray and don't hold back."

I search his eyes, looking for a way out but then they drop to his lips and I lose my resolve. I want to kiss him. I really do. But this guy, he's not good for me. It doesn't stop me though.

I lean in, pressing my lips gently to his.

It surprises me how gentle he is. After seeing what I just saw, you would never believe this guy could be gentle yet his lips are soft under mine. Tentative and explorational, waiting and asking for more.

I give. Pressing in harder with my mouth and letting my tongue follow the seam of his lips.

He makes a low rumble from his throat as his hand grips my thigh, just above my knee and he kisses me deeper, opening his mouth to let my tongue slide in.

As his tongue tangles with mine my hands come up to cup his jaw, my nails biting in slightly.

He pulls away abruptly.

"Shit, Ray."

"It's okay," I tell him softly.

My mouth is swollen and there's molten lava pooling in my stomach but I realise he needs this more than I do.

"Maybe we should head back to the table," I suggest.

He presses his forehead against mine, "Mm."

"What can I do?" I press, reaching forward to grip his hand. He snatches it back with a hiss. His knuckles are turning blue and it's the first time I've seen the blood splattered over the surface.

"Oh God," I gently pull his hand into my lap, "We need to get this looked at."

"I'm fine."

"Zach," I plead.

"Let's go."

He stands from the seat, knocking the table with his leg and then pulls me up, not waiting to see if I'm good. I'm tugged through the crowd back to our friends. Everything is as if nothing happened. Hudson looks between the two of us.

"Time to go," Zach says suddenly, "Come on."

"What's going on?" Vivi frowns, holding a fresh drink in her hand. I frown down at it.

"Is that an old fashioned?" I ask.

She shrugs, "The server just bought it over for me."

"You don't drink that," I say out loud.

"So?"

I shake my head. This night has turned out to be one of the worst of my life. I need to go home. I need to go to sleep and forget It ever happened.

"Let me see that," Zach demands, holding his hand out to Vivian to hand over the drink.

She hands it over without question and when every eye turns to me confusingly I just shake my head. I watch Zach as he holds the glass up to the dim light of the club, peering into the liquid. With a napkin, he swabs around the rim and then pours it into a nearby plant.

"Hey!" Vivian yells, "What are you doing?"

"It's time to leave."

"Come on," Hudson says to the group, "I think we've all had enough for tonight."

There's little protest as everyone gets up from the table, clearly sensing the funk that Zach's in. They have no idea.

I drop back to walk with Harper when all I really want to do is sink into Zach's side and let him take me under his arm, shielding me from whatever crazy just happened.

Sixteen

Zach

I walk Oli and Vivian into Vivian's apartment building, see them to the elevator and wait as the doors close and the light above the door tells me they're on the right floor. I head back out to the SUV. Ray sits quietly in the passenger seat whilst Harper is passed out in the back seat.

"I assume you want to go home," I don't know why I say it. It's not like I'd allow them to go anywhere else.

Ray nods, "Please."

Without another word I pull away from the sidewalk and head towards their apartment building, the only sound filling the car is Harper's soft snores.

I should try to make conversation. Talk to Ray about what happened tonight but I can hardly think straight.

For once my head isn't filled with her. It's filled with questions.

I'm missing something here. There's something more

going on than I first realised and whilst I don't know exactly what it is, I have a feeling when it's revealed it's going to knock me on my ass.

The napkin I used to swab the glass earlier is still sat in my pants pocket. There was residue around the rim. Real fine granules that wouldn't have been seen if I hadn't held it up to the light. I didn't tell them. I didn't want to worry them and without knowing *who* bought the drink, I can't be sure about whether it was sinister or not.

What I did know was that drink wasn't meant for Vivian. It was meant for Ray.

I hadn't forgotten that an old fashioned was her drink of choice. It was the drink she was sipping on the first night we met whilst Vivian slurped at sweet cocktails that ranged in colour, from pink to bright orange.

Call it a hunch if you will, my instincts are very rarely wrong, but I wasn't thinking straight and even I knew I needed to get some sleep and really process what the fuck happened tonight.

The anger is still bubbling beneath the surface and I keep replaying the image of Ray pressed up against that wall with *him* gripping her. Shit, he bruised her even though she tried to play it off. I saw the finger imprints in her arm, a light blue in colour but tomorrow they'd be dark and likely painful.

My hands curl tighter around the steering wheel, the cuts in my knuckles reopening.

It's just a reminder.

I need space.

I press harder on the pedal and make it to Ray's apartment in half the time it would usually take me. This time of night the heavy traffic was gone and the roads were clear. Thank fuck.

I park up out front and look in the mirror. Harper is

still knocked out in the back.

"I'll wake her."

I shake my head, "It's fine. I'll carry her. I'm walking you up anyway."

She doesn't argue as she pulls the door handle and steps out. She's carrying her shoes in one hand, her clutch in the other which means she's on the sidewalk without any shoes. I'd much rather carry her up, but I know that'll only cause an argument and any heat from her right now would only end up one way.

The naked kind of way.

This kind of anger, it needed a release and I didn't even get close earlier when my fists were pounding into that guys face. I need more.

I had to stop the kiss back at the club for risk of tugging up at that tiny dress and taking her right then and there.

I open the back door and lace my hands beneath her sleeping friend. She barely whimpers as I drag her from the seat and cradle her in my arms.

Ray laughs softly, "She never has been able to handle her drink."

I cock a brow, "You don't say."

Ray holds the door open for me as I carry the drunk girl inside and towards the elevator.

Harper presses her head into my chest and then mumbles in a slur of words I barely make out, "You don't make a very good pillow."

Ray bursts out laughing. I cock a brow at her, watching her as she bends at the waist and clutches her stomach as if she can't contain it.

"Why is that funny?" I ask.

"Well she's not wrong."

"No?"

"Mm-mm," She shakes her head, "You're hard. Everywhere."

Oh, you've seen nothing yet, sweetheart, I think. But tonight, isn't the night to show her. No. The first time I have her in my arms I'll make her feel special. I'll make her feel everything and then maybe I'll show her hard.

My eyes watch Ray saunter down the hallway, her bare feet light on the carpet lining the way and then she unlocks the door and guides me to Harper's bedroom.

I deposit the girl on her bed, helping Ray take off the boots on her feet before closing the door behind us.

I head straight for the door.

"Zach," Ray calls after me, "Wait."

"I've got to go, sweetheart," I tell her softly.

"Please," She murmurs.

"I'm sorry," I tell her honestly, "I can't."

"Why?" she demands.

I pause at the door, one hand on the handle.

"Do you regret kissing me? Is that why?"

My head tips back. "God no."

"Then why?"

I spin on her, closing the gap between us, feeling my frustration bubbling right back to the surface,

"Because, Ray. If I stay, I'm going to fuck you. I'm going to fuck you hard and not soft or gentle the way you deserve for the first time I have you. You deserve more than that and so I am going to leave. I'm going to go home and beat the shit out of sandbag and then next week, we can talk."

Her head snaps back but I don't miss the heat that rises in her eyes. Not the fire I'm used to when she's about to snap back at me. No this is desire. Raw. Undiluted and so fucking tempting it's taking everything I have not to just strip her right now.

"Goodnight, Ray," I growl out.

I don't even kiss her.

"Fuck!" I yell as I step out on the sidewalk, my voice echoing down the empty streets. "Fuck!"

This is so fucked up.

I speed my way back to the condo.

I don't even strip from the suit when I make my way through to my gym, a bag already strung up. My fists slam into the side. Pain explodes over my knuckles, but I don't stop. One. Two. I slam my hands into the sides of it over and over again.

He touched her.

He hurt her.

I'm missing something. Something so fucking detrimental that I feel like an idiot for missing it and yet my mind can't quite follow the lines. It can't work out the path and at the end of it, at the end of whatever fucking nightmare this is, someone's going to get hurt. A part of the reason I agreed to come into the family business was because I was able to see the bigger picture. It was something trained into me at a young age. I never looked at something and saw face value, I was always able to see deeper than that and work out exactly what was going on but this, it was like there was this screen of fog stopping me from seeing any further ahead.

Was it because of Ray?

Was she stopping me from being able to see anything clearly?

Even if it were, would I be able to stop?

I doubted it. She was well and truly under my skin. Nah, she was deeper than that. She was rooted to my bones. I felt her inside me, I heard her voice and I saw her big blues every time I closed my eyes. I could smell her like a ghost passing by and feel her hands, small and dainty on my skin.

I stop punching and grip it, stopping it from swinging like a pendulum and then I press my forehead against the leather, taking deep steadying breaths.

What the hell was I going to do about this?

What I really needed to do was sleep. I needed a clear head, but sleep wouldn't come for me tonight.

With some of my tension worked from my system I head through to the shower and stand beneath it for so long the water starts to run cold and then I stay in some more.

I'll take anything that'll take away this feeling. Anything.

Seventeen

Zach

"Can you help me or not?" I hiss down the line, "I need this tested as soon as possible."

"Where did you even get it?" The voice on the other line says. He's a friend of the company, a guy with the means to an end. He can get me the results of the residue I swiped from the glass without asking me any questions.

"Your job isn't to ask questions," I snap, "When can I get the result?"

"A week if you send it to me Monday."

"Done."

I don't wait for a response. I slam my cell down on to the desk and start to write out the address where I'm sending the napkin. I've placed it in a clear sealed plastic bag and just hope there's enough there to get a clear result.

I'm almost a hundred percent about what it is but I

want it confirmed.

Scott, my brother, won't like this at all but what he doesn't know won't hurt him. He's done shit in the past that I haven't agreed with.

I place the parcel to the side, ready to be sent on Monday and then turn my attention back to the emails filling my work account. This is why I had taken myself out the field for some time, the admin that comes with running a business is so much more than I ever expected and with my fatigue I can hardly see the words on the screen.

I didn't sleep at all last night. I tried. I called one of my other guys in to watch Vivian today. She didn't have much on, just a few visits to her family but we needed someone with her at all times with everything that's going. As far as I could tell Ray wasn't with her.

I wonder what she's doing today. It's early on a Saturday morning and I want to know what she does in her own time. Who is she when she isn't, Ray, Vivian's assistant? What is she like behind a closed door?

She has her quirks, I know that with the sassy mugs she carries around with her and from what I've seen of her apartment she's all about empowerment, which I completely dig. I want to dig deep and unearth everything.

Unable to focus on the emails I grab my swim trunks and head down to the onsite swimming pool.

Would I have still signed up for this if I had known the shit that came with it?

Probably. It wasn't the job I wanted.

I realise that now.

It was Ray I wanted, and I would have taken her any way I could have. It's the wrong way to go around it but since that first meeting back in the bar all those weeks ago, I haven't been able to think about another woman since.

I really wish I knew what it was that had me so entrapped.

After my swim I dry off and head back upstairs, pulling on a pair of jeans and a shirt, leaving it unbuttoned. I wasn't planning on going anywhere today so I was choosing comfort over anything else. My phone is flashing with a new notification, so I unlock it to find a text from Ray.

What are you doing?

Just some work. I reply.

Can I come over?

Now?

Yes.

Why did she want to come over?

I mean sure, do you need something?

What's your address?

I send her the address to the apartment building and then repeat my question. Why would she want to come here? She doesn't respond but twenty minutes later the buzzer sounds and Ray's voice trickles in through the speaker. I buzz her up and then go to the door, opening it ready for when she makes it up the three floors to my condo.

I see her dark head of hair coming up the stairs. It's down, curling around her pretty face and she's bare of any makeup. She's wearing a cute little pair of cut off shorts with sneakers and a t-shirt that's knotted in the front to show off her toned midriff.

Her eyes go wide when she spots me in the doorway, her gaze snagging on my chest which is still on show seeing as I haven't done the buttons of my shirt up. I lean on the doorframe and cross my arms, letting my eyes take in her long, tanned legs.

"What can I do for you?" I ask.

My eyes fall to her lips, remembering how they felt under mine last night. I can still taste the champagne from her tongue.

"I bought coffee," She shoves out a take-away cup, keeping one back for herself.

"Thanks, did you come all the way over here to bring me coffee?"

"No," she shakes her head, "I wanted to talk. About last night."

As she says it, she looks to my hand which I'd bandaged up after my swim. The knuckles are swollen and bruised but I've dealt with worse and nothing's broken. I can't say the same for that Sam guy. I *hope* something is broken for him.

I tuck the hand under my arm, hiding it from her.

Whilst Sam got everything he deserved, I didn't like that she saw that side of me. I fought a lot during my teenage years, underground fights that were on the wrong side of the law. It gave me a rush, but it's been a long time since I've used my fists on another body. I choose to use a bag rather than a face nowadays, less mess that way and with the business, it wouldn't exactly be good for the company if I were caught.

"What about it?" I grumble.

"Can I come in?" She looks past my shoulder and I step back, pushing the door open wider. She offers me a small smile as she ducks beneath my arm and into my space. Her scent blows under my nose and I inhale, finding my eyes falling closed.

This woman was dangerous.

She was going to destroy me, and she didn't even realise it.

She wants to be rocked but I think maybe it's me she's about to be knocked on their ass.

"This is nice," Ray looks around the clean living room, eyes roaming over my dark furniture and natural accents. A large TV has been mounted to the wall with a huge sound system beneath it. I don't know why I bought it. I never actually watch TV. Too busy doing other shit with my time. Nice wouldn't be what I called it. Sterile maybe. Other than the furniture in here I hadn't added anything.

"Ray," I cock a brow and take a sip of my coffee, "What did you come here for?"

She walks to the wall of windows that looks down onto the city, "Wow, great view."

"Ray."

"Hey, you can see the beach from here."

"No, you can't."

She runs a hand over her face, "I wanted to thank you."

"For what?"

"That thing with Sam last night," she shakes her head, "Of course, I wish you didn't get hurt."

"I didn't."

"Your hands," she points out.

"A scratch."

She scoffs, "Anyway, thank you."

"You came all the way out here to say thank you?"

"Well," she suddenly looks uncomfortable, "I also wanted to ask you out."

Floored.

"What?"

"Do you want to go out with me? To dinner or something?"

"Are you asking me out on a date?" My mouth curls

into a smug smile and I start to make my way towards her, my head cocked to the side.

"Uh," she stammers, stepping back. She doesn't go far, her back hits the window and before she can go anywhere else I'm in front of her, looking down into those big blues, "Not a date. A thank you."

"Sounds like a date to me," I say in a low voice. I feel her presence in the way the air pushes into me, even though I'm not touching her. Yet.

"No, no date." She shakes her head, pupils huge. She drops her gaze to my bare chest, her eyes tracing the outlines of the ink I have across my pecs and ribs.

"What if I asked you on a date?" I drop my head, running the tip of my nose down the column of her throat. She tips her head to the side, allowing me access.

Well this changes things. "Would you say yes?"

She nods her head subtly.

"What if I asked to kiss you again? Would you say yes?" I press my lips to the skin just below her ear.

A little whimper sounds from her lips and the noise goes straight to my cock.

She nods again.

"Now?"

"Zach," she pleads.

I slam my mouth down on hers, her lips opening for me immediately. My tongue pushes in. Our teeth clash, our hands grab. This isn't like any of the other kisses. This is hot, urgent. Without breaking the kiss, I take her coffee and place it on the side before coming back to grab her hips, pulling her into me roughly.

She groans as I push my throbbing cock into her lower belly. Her fingernails bite into the skin on my abdomen, my muscles jumping under her touch.

"Holy shit," I growl before reaching behind her

thighs, just below her ass and lifting her. Her legs wrap around my hips.

"Did you come all the way over here to let me fuck you, Ray?" I ask against her lips. "Is that what you want?"

"Shit, Zach," She grinds her hips against the hard length in my jeans, "You told me." She stutters

"Told you what, sweetheart?"

"You told me you wanted to last night, that you wanted it hard."

I growl, "I did."

"Maybe I want it hard too?"

I groan, "Shit, Ray, you're going to kill me."

"I'm done fighting it," she moans as my lips feather down her neck, teeth grazing across her collar bones, "I'm done fighting this thing."

"About time!"

Still holding her against me, I pull her away from the window and head towards my bedroom, my mouth exploring every place it can reach, her jaw, neck, ears and she lets me. Her arms loop around my neck, the heels of her feet digging into my lower back. She's soft under my fingers, her ass moulding around my fingertips.

I kick the bedroom door open and not so subtly drop her onto the mattress.

"I hope you didn't have plans today," I tell her, eyes following the lines of her body as she spreads out on my bed, "Because I'm not letting you go."

Eighteen

Zach

I drag my hand from her ankle up her shin, over the knee and to her thigh, my fingers whisper over the sensitive skin on the inside. I've never seen something so beautiful. She watches me from beneath hooded lids, her plump lips parted slightly.

I kneel down between her thighs, my hands running over the denim of her shorts until I find the button and flick my fingers, popping it open.

I can see a trace of pink lace and just that has my mouth watering.

"Lift," I order, tapping her hip. She does as I ask, propping herself up as I hook my fingers into the waist band of her shorts and drag them down her thighs. I throw them over my shoulder, eyes drinking in that pink lacy thong that barely covers her.

"Take your top off," I tell her, sitting back on my

heels.

Hooking her fingers beneath the hem, she tugs it over her head, leaving her in a little lacy bra that matches her panties. There's barely anything to it, just a thin piece of material that's entirely see-through. Her nipples are peaked, rosy in colour and unable to stop myself, I lean in, sucking one into my mouth through the lace. Her back bows off the bed and I slip a hand beneath her, holding her against me as my tongue swirls and my teeth nip.

Having her skin against mine, it's like nothing I've ever felt. Her warmth seeps through me, setting soul deep.

"Zach," she moans.

Leaving her nipple, I move down over her ribs, kissing her flesh, my hand splayed out over her sternum. God my hands look good on her. My knuckles brush her clit through the material of her thong and holy shit she's *wet* for me. I feel it through the thin lace.

"I'll buy you a new pair," I tell her and before she can question it, I snap the thin band that holds her underwear in place. My mouth closes around her, her arousal hot on my tongue.

She cries out and I feel a grin tugging at my mouth, my tongue flicking against her sensitive nub.

I add my fingers, pushing into her and her knees fall apart, her hips moving so she grinds against my face.

"Fuck, sweetheart," I rumble against her, "You taste even better than I imagined."

"Zach, I can't," she moans desperately.

"Oh, you can," I suck her into my mouth and pulse my fingers feeling her muscles begin to spasm. She's climbing and I'm determined to push her over the edge, to have her falling apart under my touch.

"Yes, yes," she chants, "Oh *god!*"

She throws her head back as her climax grips her, her muscles tensing up as her legs clamp around my ears.

I'm chuckling when I come back up and yeah, I might just be a little smug right now. Wasn't it her own words saying she's never had an orgasm by someone else before?

"Don't get cocky," she breathes, hooded eyes looking up at me.

She pushes up onto her elbows, reaching forward to press a kiss to my chest. My eyes fall closed, my skin overly sensitive. I shrug off my shirt and then stand, hands going to the button fly of my jeans. Her eyes watch me, her tongue darting out to wet her kiss swollen bottom lip.

"Keep looking at me like that, sweetheart and it won't just be today I don't let you go."

"Promises, promises," she retorts, her eyes never leaving my hands as pop one button at a time.

"Take them off," I challenge.

One brow twitches and she sits up, sliding her hands under the waistband of my jeans. As she tugs them down, she licks her tongue up my abs. My chin hits my chest as I watch her, my cock straining to be free.

When I'm finally free I don't have a chance to do anything. She sucks the crown of my cock into her mouth, her tongue flicking over the tip.

"Fuck!" I yell, my hands balling into fists at my sides. My hips move off their own accord, pulsing back and forth as she hollows out her cheeks and sucks me to the back of throat.

I need to be in her. I need to claim her, every inch of her. Pulling out of her mouth I kick off my jeans and kneel at the end of the bed. She begins to scoot up the mattress, her eyes never leaving mine. Fuck she's beautiful. My hands fall to her hips and I squeeze, bringing her ass off the bed until she's almost in my lap.

"I've thought about this," I admit, eyes taking in all her nakedness. "Too much and too often."

"Zach," she whispers as I feather a finger up her centre. Her lashes flutter closed. I'm so fucking hard for her it hurts. Not wanting to take another minute, I lean over and grab a condom from the nightstand, sheathing myself quickly before I line the head of my cock up with her entrance. The warmth of her rushes up my shaft and I have to push down the need to just pound forward and claim her. Her tightness squeezes me as I push in slowly. Her breath comes out in a whoosh and her fists ball up the sheets beneath her.

"Look at me," I demand, "Open your eyes."

Her lids open and she meets my gaze, the blues so dark, laced with desire and I'm sure mine match. I push in further, fighting every instinct to fuck her hard and rough, until I'm in to the hilt. I groan, letting the sensations of her around me settle in.

With my hands on her hips I bring myself back and then slide in again. A little whimper escapes her lips and it only spurs me on. I speed up, pulling out and then pushing back in, feeling her muscles spasm.

I can feel my patience snapping, my willpower slipping away and my fingers squeeze hard enough to bruise.

"Keep doing that," Ray moans, "God, yes."

Pride fills my chest at the pleasure etched into her face. I want to puff out and grunt like a fucking caveman because I've got this pretty girl under me. She's riding the train of pleasure because of me.

And that does it for me.

"Fuck Ray," I lean forward, grab her leg and bring it up to rest on my shoulder as I really go to work. I pound into her again and again, hard, the only sound filling the room is her pleasured cries of ecstasy and skin slapping against skin. I want her to come on my cock. I want to feel her release take her and her muscles bunch around me.

I circle her clit with my thumb and she goes wild, her head tipping back as her hips lift off the bed. I push her back down, my fingers splayed over her stomach.

I feel the start of her orgasm, I feel it in the way her muscles quiver and her legs go tense and then she's freefalling. She squeezes me so fucking tight it's a vice around my shaft.

"Shit," I hiss through my teeth, her own release drawing mine from me. I ride it out, holding her to me as my climax quakes through my body. I drop down onto the bed next to her.

We lay there in silence for a few minutes, both staring up at the ceiling whilst our breathing steadies back out. When I look over to her, her eyes are closed so I take a minute to peruse her naked body, realising she's still in that lacy bra, even if the cups have been dragged down and are now sitting beneath her ample breasts.

God there isn't a single thing wrong with her, not her silky skin or round breasts, not her taut stomach or long toned legs. As if sensing my eyes on her, her own open and she turns to look at me.

"Hi," she breathes.

"Hi."

"Believe it or not," she giggles, "I didn't actually come over for that. I did only come to thank you."

I pull off the condom, tie it off and throw it in the

trash before I turn back to her, "I'm gonna ask you a question." My smile is bright and devious, "were you *rocked?*"

Nineteen

Ray

I feel the blood heat my cheeks before I can mask the embarrassment. I had forgotten he'd heard that drunken confession all those weeks ago. I choose to play this off. He's teasing me. Maybe it's time I tease him back.

I shrug my shoulders nonchalantly, "Well I mean, it was okay."

Truthfully, he had *rocked* me. That was the best sex I'd ever had and not because of the two orgasms he gave me. It was true, I'd never had an orgasm at the hand – or mouth – and cock – as it were, by a man. I was no saint and I'd had lovers, but no one ever came close to getting me off, not like he just did. Shit I saw stars. I can still feel the remnants of the pleasure in my veins, lighting my nerves on fire.

The way he touched me, gah, he knew exactly what

he was doing. He was possessive and claiming and just so fucking dominating. The way his hands held my hips as he worked in and out of me, the way his eyes watched where our bodies joined like he couldn't miss a single second of it.

"You little liar," he growls and before I realise it, he's grabbed me and I'm straddling him, his already hardening cock pressing against my clit. Almost as if reflex, my hips glide me up and down his shaft. His eyes roll back as his fingers bite into my thighs.

"Liar? Me? Never," I gasp in mock offence, "How could you say such a thing."

"I fucking rocked you," he growls, lifting his hips to apply more pressure to my already sensitive centre. How was the man getting hard again? He'd only just finished! "I fucking know I did, if it wasn't the way you clenched around my cock," his words send a bolt of heat between my legs, "Then it was definitely your screams of pleasure."

"It was hardly a scream," I scoff.

"You reckon?" He grins, reaching over to the nightstand to pull another foil wrapper from the drawer, "Well maybe I should try harder."

He's sheathed in seconds and pushing into me. I'm already so wet for him he just slides in and I find my seat in his lap, my hips rocking as I draw him and out of my body.

"God you feel so good, sweetheart," He tells me.

I grind into him and his hands come up to squeeze my breasts, pinching my nipples between his thumb and forefinger.

I throw my head back, finding a rhythm as I ride him, sliding up and down his cock like my life depended on it.

"Fuck you're beautiful riding me like that," Zach praises, suddenly sitting and wrapping his muscular arms around my middle. I swear his arms could go round me twice and with this new position it's harder to keep my pace, but I somehow manage it, even with his head buried in my breasts and my hands on his shoulders.

It's not long before my third orgasm is building, and my walls clamp down around his cock. I cry out, unable to stop myself as my climax rips through me. He follows soon after and then when we're done, we collapse down on the bed, me draped over his chest, him still buried deep inside me.

His hand brushes down my spine soothingly, toying with the ends of my hair and twirling it around his fingertips.

I listen to his heartbeat, thumping steadily in his chest and inhale his scent. It's so masculine, so Zach that I could bottle it and make millions. Eventually he pulls out of me, takes off the condom and throws it into the trash.

An hour or so passes like that, me curled into his side, our breathing the only noise in the room. It isn't awkward or tense, it's…comfortable. Like this is how it's supposed to be. My own body, traitorous as it is, disrupts the tranquillity by growling with hunger.

I'd skipped breakfast, too tense from the events of last night to eat anything and then I'd skipped lunch in favour of coming here.

And I do not regret that decision one bit.

He chuckles, "Let me make you something."

I don't hide my surprise, "You cook?"

"Mm," he nods, tapping my chin, "Kinda had to if I wanted to eat growing up."

My frown must be question enough because he

proceeds to answer.

"It was just me, my brother, Scott, and my dad. My mom took off when I was about six months old. We learned to cook when we were tall enough to reach the stove."

"Oh," what do I say to that?

"Come on," He presses a kiss to my lips. He pulls on his jeans – without underwear – which is so stupidly sexy and throws his shirt at me. I was so busy ogling the Adonis in front of me that I didn't see it coming and it hits me in the face.

I grab the expensive material and glare at him. His eyes crinkle with mirth. "Ass."

I slip it on over my shoulders and button it up before sliding off the bed and heading to his en-suite. "I'll meet you in the kitchen." I tell him over my shoulder and then close the door, stopping in front of the mirror.

I'm shocked at what I find staring back at me. I mean it's not that I look bad, well fucked maybe. My hair is a mess, my neck red with subtle bite marks and my eyes are wild, my lips curved into a perpetual smile.

I do my business and then splash some water on my face, taking a few deep breaths. It was just sex. Just. Sex. Don't think into it too much.

I hear oil sizzling when I start down the hall and music on low. Zach stands in the kitchen, the muscles in his back flexing with whatever he's doing with his hands. The ink from his arms and chest continues on his back and he has those dimples in the base of his spine. He also has a great ass, really, you could bounce a quarter off of it. I'd noticed it in his suit before, but I'd also felt it under the heels of my feet as I urged him on whilst he was slamming into me, again and again.

Heat floods me at the memory. Shit, it was only earlier.

I shake my head to clear the fog and step into the kitchen. "What are you making?"

"Omelettes," He shrugs.

I nod and perch on the stool at the table, looking around the condo. It's spacious but just a little empty. There're no photos on the walls, nothing personal hanging around, not even any books. It's almost like he's not planning on sticking around.

"What's going on in that pretty head of yours?" He asks, placing a plate in front of me.

"You don't have anything personal out."

He sits next to me with his own food and digs in, "I haven't had time. I have bunch of stuff in storage but just haven't had the time to get it all out yet."

I nod, "So you're planning to stick around then?"

"Well we have just opened an office here and someone needs to run it," he says, amused.

I nod again. The light outside has started to dim and I reluctantly look at the clock hanging on the walls.

"I should go," I say after the last bite of food.

"Stay," he says, reaching out to curl his fingers around mine.

Just. Sex.

"No, it's okay, I've actually got to get up early tomorrow and Harper will wonder where I am.".

His dark brows pull down and he releases my hand, "Okay."

"Thanks for this," I gesture to the plate and place it in the sink before making my way back to the bedroom. I start searching for my clothes, finding them in various places around the room. My shorts are hanging off the side of a dresser, my top has been kicked under the bed and my shoes are on opposites sides of the room. I also find my underwear or what's left of them anyway. I hold the ripped fabric off my finger, the material shredded. Damn it, this was a set. Commando it is. I pull my shorts on over my legs, not entirely enjoying the feel of the denim against my bare flesh and then tug my tee over my head.

When I come back out into the main living area, Zach's at the sink, rinsing the plates.

I find my purse and pull out my phone, ordering an uber.

"I'll see you Monday?" I ask, suddenly feeling awkward. What do we do from here? Hug? Kiss? Fuck, I have no idea.

"Yeah," he picks up a cloth and wipes his hands on it, leaning back on the counter. His eyes do a sweep of my body, "You're not wearing panties."

My face flushes, "No. you destroyed them."

His jaw goes tight.

My phone buzzes, letting me know my driver is waiting. I make a beeline for the door.

Shit this was not what I had expected and now that's done and over, I can't help but feel like we just made a mistake.

Just because there's heat between us doesn't mean we should have acted on it. People are attracted to one another all the time, it doesn't mean you should fall into bed with them and it's not like we actually get along.

I feel like we've just made things so much worse.

No, we can be adults about this. I doubt he cares much. He got me in his bed. What was it he said to me that first day we met? That he would have fucked and left.

We can act like this never happened.

I'm just climbing into the back of the uber when I hear my name being called behind me. I look out the window, searching for the owner when I see Zach stepping out the doors of his building, his hands buried in his pockets. He follows me as the uber pulls away from the sidewalk and is still there when we turn the corner at the end of the street. I only turn back when I can no longer see him.

What the fuck do we do now?

Twenty

Ray

Monday morning comes round and the nerves I had managed to keep buried swarm to the surface. I haven't heard from Zach since Saturday. I had gone to text him a few times but then I told myself off and threw my phone across the room.

God what was I? In high school?

Taking a deep breath, I pull my pants over my legs. They're navy blue with white pin stripes and they fit me like a glove, moulding to the shape of my legs and hips. I pair it with a white blouse and my white heels, leaving my hair down but only because of the faded blue bruises on my neck. I was fielding questions from Harper all day yesterday I could only imagine what Vivian would be like should she see them. That girl was like a dog with a bone if she thought she was missing out on something.

Harper is still sleeping when I step out into the kitchen and taking the silence, I quickly make a coffee whilst I order an uber and then step out into the hall. I don't have the stomach to deny, deny, deny. I hated lying to my friends, but this wasn't really lying. This was just hiding something from them that I know will only bring more questions. They'll be disappointed when I tell them it was only sex. Because that's all it was.

It was great sex. Mind blowing sex in fact, but it wouldn't go any further than that. My body ached for him and *because* of him but I could push that down. I wouldn't be that needy girl. I'll just go back to my normal self.

I sip my coffee as I wait for my uber, browsing social media.

My senses prickle. It's an awareness, a feeling you get when you know someone is watching you. I look up from my phone and scan the sidewalk. Whilst we're still in a busy part of the city this is a residential street so it's quiet with only a few others milling around and no one here is paying me any attention.

My hands get clammy with nerves and I'm just debating stepping back in the building when a silver Toyota pulls up in front of me and my phone pings to let me know my driver is here. I check the car matches the details on the screen and when they do, I climb in the back and greet my driver. He smiles at me warmly and then we make our way to Vivian's apartment.

"Thanks," I tell him and climb out, heading into the building quickly. In the elevator ride up I check over Vivi's schedule. We have a morning at a studio for a shoot she's doing for a cosmetics company, but the afternoon is free. Huh. That hardly ever happens.

"Good morning!" Vivi yells animatedly from the

kitchen where she's blitzing something in her blender.

"Hi," I smile, placing my items on her side. "Good weekend?"

"The best, it was so good to see my family, thank you for making sure I could do that."

I shrug, "That's alright."

"What did you do?" She asks, pouring the green concoction into a large glass.

Had sex. Hot wild sex. "Not much."

No one had mentioned Friday night. Not me, not Harper, Oli or Vivi. It was a subject we were just choosing to ignore. They got the jist of it, but no questions were asked and that's the way we are going to keep it. I don't need to rehash every detail about what happened with Sam. That guy scared the hell out of me. Not that I like to admit it. Being scared of someone gave them power and he didn't deserve that.

He was just persistent and demanding and couldn't take no for an answer. I shiver at the thought of what could have happened if Zach hadn't arrived. I was in a packed club and other than that one girl who stopped to check in on me, no one batted an eyelid. Would he have been able to get me out of there, kicking and screaming?

Who knows. But I definitely never want to find out.

I wrinkle my nose as Vivian chugs back her drink, wiping her mouth with the back of her hand.

The buzzer at the door rings, "Miss Prescott, Miss Stone, Mr Wyatt is here to collect you. He told me to let you know he'll be waiting outside."

"That's weird," Vivian frowns, "He always comes up."

I shrug and inwardly groan. Was he going to make this awkward now?

We grab our things and head down, finding Zach exactly where he said he would be. He stands casually by the back door of the SUV, his suit pristine and freshly pressed, his silver eyes hidden behind a pair of sunglasses. The button of his suit jacket is done up around the middle and it looks like his shoes have recently been shined. These were all details I never picked up on before. Like how the sun gave his hair an almost reddish tinge even though it was black and how his hands looked linked together in front of his abdomen like that.

God those hands. They were so skilled. I loved the way he held me down with them, his fingers splayed across my skin.

"Good morning, Vivian," He greets as he opens the back door, "Ray."

"Zach," I try for confident but get a squeak.

His lips twitch.

Fuck.

Vivian climbs into the back of the car. Either she's completely oblivious to the tension between us or she's hiding it well. As I climb into the back of the car Zach's hand brushes down my spine.

My head whips back to him but he's already moving to close the door behind me. A mistake. He didn't actually mean to touch me. It doesn't stop the hum in my veins from turning from a soft lull to a full blown choir though.

I glue my eyes to my screen as we make the drive over to the studio. Vivian is happily discussing what she did at the weekend with her family and Zach's fully invested in the conversation, laughing along with her stories about her crazy family but me? I'm dying inside.

His laugh does weird things to me. My lady bits have

definitely taken notice of the deep rumble and how it seeps beneath my skin and squeezes my organs.

I try to be subtle about my escape from the car but when I get nervous or flustered, I get clumsy and as I step from the car I misjudge the distance from the car to the sidewalk and the next thing I know I'm on my ass on the concrete.

For a minute I sit, legs splayed, completely dazed, wondering what the fuck just happened.

Two legs donned in suit pants appear in front of me and I squint up to find Zach looking down at me, his lips subtly pulled into an amused smile.

"You alright down there?"

"Oh yeah," I wave a hand like I wanted to fall on my ass, "Just getting comfy."

He offers me a hand and I take it, snatching it back as soon as I find my feet and stop trying to impersonate Bambi. At least Bambi looked cute when he slipped on ice. I just look like an idiot.

"I like those pants," Zach says in my ear as I stride past him. I look back at him, seeing his eyes are on my ass rather than my face.

I narrow my eyes. He's just fucking with me. My thoughts are backed up by the amusement lighting up his silver eyes.

I walk with Vivian into the building, sign us in and head through to the dressing rooms. I stay tucked away safely behind that door whilst Zach waits outside. I know my haven will only last so long as when Vivi goes off for the shoot we'll have to stick to the side-lines so I won't be able to use her as my own personal safety net but I'll deal with that when it comes to it.

"You're a free woman this afternoon," I tell Vivian,

crossing my legs and shutting off the tablet.

"Oo," her eyes light up, "I could really use a shopping trip and a gossip."

My eyes widen. What did she know!?

"Something happened Friday and I really need to talk to you about it."

"Between whom?" I squeak.

"Hudson and me," she pulls her lip into her teeth and then releases it when the makeup artists glares at her, "Sorry," she mumbles.

"Oh," I sag with relief.

"Why, do you have something too?"

"Me? *No!*"

Her eyes narrow at me in the mirror so I quickly change the subject, "Shopping sounds good."

"Okay good."

"Right, hon, you're all set."

I do a good job of ignoring Zach as we make it to the set but then Vivi is swept away and we're left alone at the back of the large room.

He's like a goddamn building next to me and he's close to me too. I mean there's so much space around us, he could literally stand anywhere and yet he's choosing to loom over me.

"Why are you ignoring me?" He quizzes, keeping his gaze trained on the photoshoot happening up ahead.

"I'm not."

Nonchalant. I've got this.

"Sure you are, sweetheart, I can't really figure out why though."

"No, I'm just trying to be normal, you know before…" I trail off.

"We fucked."

I suck in a sharp breath, "Yeah."

"Why do you want normalcy?"

"So, it's not weird?"

He chuckles, "You're making it a little strange, Ray. I mean we're two consenting adults."

"I know that, but I don't want you to think I'm like hanging off you."

"I wouldn't mind," he smirks, "But I also don't really want normal."

My head snaps towards him, "You don't?"

He scoffs, "No, Ray."

"Then what do you want?"

"You."

Twenty-one

Zach

Áll that tension she's been harbouring in her little body rushes out and her eyes flash, the blue turning electric.

"I don't understand," she stammers, "You got me in bed. That was the goal, right?"

"Jesus Christ, Ray, what do you take me for?"

She shrugs innocently, dragging that plump bottom lip between her teeth.

Using the pad of my thumb I pull it out, "The goal wasn't just to get you into bed. It might have been at the beginning but now…"

"Now?"

"I want to take you out, you know," shit now I was nervous, "for dinner."

"Wait you were serious?"

"Yes, Ray, shit," I drag a hand through my hair, "I

want to take you out."

"Okay."

"Yeah?"

She nods shyly, "I'd like that."

I step closer, not like there was much space between us to begin with, and she seemingly melts into my side.

"Is that why you rushed out of my place on Saturday?" It's been nagging at me since she made her escape.

"I guess so."

I shake my head, "I'm not that kind of guy, Ray. I may have said some shit to you but that was just me being an asshole."

"Is that not your default function?" She jokes.

"Ha ha," I cock a brow, "You forget what all that heat you throw my way does to me."

Her eyes drop to my crotch and her eyes widen. Truth be told I was already getting hard at her proximity but that sass, shit that lights me on fire.

"Here!?"

"You underestimate me, sweetheart," I tease, grazing the tip of my finger down the side of her face, "That's dangerous."

"You're dangerous."

"You have no idea."

—

"Let's get some late lunch," Vivi exclaims as we hit the main shopping strip in downtown LA. Ray nods, darting a look over her shoulder at me. I follow the girls to a little café off the main sidewalk. It's cute, with little round tables and chequered tablecloths and the smell of fresh coffee and fried food. It wasn't the type of place I saw either of these two eating at but they're full of surprises.

I realise that none of the girls of this group fit into any type of norm and that's not necessarily a bad thing.

"Table for three," Vivian tells the hostess.

"Oh no," I try to refuse but she glares at me and I hold my hands up in surrender.

The hostess shows us to a little table at the back of the café, hands us some menus and then disappears to seat a couple who have just walked through the door.

Ray is hiding behind the menu.

"I don't know why you bother," Vivian laughs, putting her finger on top of the menu and pushing it down until her sweet little face is revealed. "You get the same every time we're here."

"I like to check for new items," she pouts.

Vivian rolls her eyes and then faces me, "The fish here is amazing."

"Then I'll get the fish," I agree.

I'm supposed to be working. Not dining out but I'm not going to lie and say I hate how close I am to Ray right now. Her knee brushes mine beneath the table and with the cover of the cloth, I'm able to drop my hand beneath and trail a hand up her thigh. I'm sorry she's wearing pants rather than a dress or a skirt, but she still flushes at my touch and I love how she reacts to me.

Her hand slaps down on top of mine and she grips me, her fingernails biting in a little, stopping me from getting any further up.

Her pupils are huge, the blue of her eyes dark and I can see the pulse point jumping wildly in her throat.

As much as I love sparring with the woman because that sass does things to me, now that I've had her, tasted her, *claimed* her, all I want is to do it all over again.

As Neanderthal as it is, I want the whole fucking city – no the whole fucking world to know she is *mine*.

I was keeping her.

I hide my smirk behind my hand just as the waitress comes to take our orders.

"So," Vivian starts, "I kissed Hudson."

Ray almost chokes on her water, but she manages to keep it in, pressing her napkin to her lips. "What?"

"Friday night. I kissed him."

Why was this a big deal? Vivian rolls her eyes at me and pointedly ignores me as she looks back to her friend. Right girl talk.

"I'm just going to go to the bathroom," I tell the two of them, "Reckon you can stay out of trouble?"

"Yes," Vivi grumbles.

I'm gone maybe a few minutes but when I come back to the table, Ray has lost all colour in her cheeks and she's staring down at her tablet. Vivian looks glum.

"What happened?" I demand, looking over Ray's shoulder. My hand instinctively curls around her shoulder, my thumb circling.

"We got another email," Vivian answers for her.

I stare down at the screen.

I saw the kiss. I saw it all.

How could you do that to us?

We have something special.

I warned you. I WARNED YOU.

This fucker was seriously unhinged. But why would he wait until now to send this message. I look around the restaurant. He could be here right now. Watching her. Maybe he waited so he could see her reaction to the email.

Everything in my head was still snagging on that Declan guy but I had nothing solid to go on. I had sent the napkin off for testing this morning, but it'll be a couple of days before I get those results back. He was there Friday to see the kiss between Vivian and Hudson.

"Where did it happen?" I turn to Vivian.

"I didn't think anyone saw," she says in a small voice, "It was just off of the bathrooms. It was when he was walking me back. You and Ray had disappeared at this point."

Yeah, I was probably either beating the shit out of some guy or groping her in a booth. It'll probably be the latter because if she was near the bathrooms, she would have seen me laying into the guy.

"If he was at the club," I tell her, "He would have had eyes on you at all times. He certainly wouldn't have missed you getting cosy with Hudson."

"Zach!" Ray chastises.

"What?" What'd I do?

Ray shakes her head, "We need to go see Hudson. He'll want to know about this."

"Thing is," Vivian fidgets, "We haven't talked since then and I think he may regret it."

"Your pride might have to take a hit on this one." I say.

Ray glares at me.

Okay maybe I just need to shut up.

"What does he mean, he warned me?" Vivian asks

"The threats to the people you love," Ray clarifies.

Vivian's eyes widen, "Shit, this is just like an episode of *pretty little liars.*"

What? Is this chick on drugs?

Ray shakes her head, "Not the time, Vivi."

"You're right, well let's go then. The sooner we go

146

see Hudson the sooner I can go drown in a bottle of
wine."

Twenty-two

Zach

I escort the girls back to the SUV, my instincts screaming at me to get them the fuck out of there, not just Vivian, Ray too. I had a feeling she was somehow tied into all of this. How? I didn't know. Her face is void of any colour, that spark I saw in her eyes earlier diminished and I fucking hated it. I hated that despite her cool exterior, she was terrified. Of a man hiding behind a computer. And if I knew anything about Ray, she wasn't afraid for herself. She was afraid for Vivian and Harper and Oli. She'd already been the target of his anger once, the chances are she wouldn't be again, no, the fucker will likely go after one of the other girls now to prove a point.

"Can you get hold of Harper and Oli?" I ask after I climb in the front seat, "Just tell them to keep an eye out and call the cops if they see anything suspicious."

Ray nods and begins to tap away on her phone as I

pull into the heavy LA traffic.

As I drive I notice a car has been tailing us since we pulled away from the café. A simple black sedan but the front screen is completely tinted and with the glare of the afternoon sun, it's impossible to see the driver. I turn a corner, they follow and again at the end of the street.

"Shit," I murmur, I don't want to worry the girls. "Looks like road works," I lie, "I'm just going to take a detour."

I need to figure out if this guy is actually a tail. I mean the chances of another car going in the exact same direction is pretty slim, but this could also be my paranoia getting the better of me.

"Road works?" Ray questions, "I didn't realise they were doing work down here. Nothing is posted."

I shrug, "Perhaps they forgot."

Yeah right. I'm going to need to lie better than that.

"Maybe," Ray answers, narrowing her eyes at me.

Yeah sweetheart, I know. I'm a shitty liar.

I divert to the highway, heading away from the city and come off the slip to circle back round. The car stays on my heels.

Fuck.

Definitely following us.

I lean back in my chair and flick my eyes to the mirrors, trying to check for plates but of course, there are none.

"Where are you going?" Ray leans forward, placing herself between the seats. Her shoulder brushes mine and I feel her eyes boring into the side of my face.

God did she need to be such a distraction.

"Detour," I shrug nonchalantly.

Without another choice I head towards the offices,

keeping one eye on the car behind us. When we pull up and park, I throw myself out, ready to take on whoever it is but instead of coming to a stop with me, they speed on by, too quick for me to get a good look at the driver.

"What's your problem?" Ray comes around to my side of the car, her hands planted on her hips.

"Nothing, sweetheart," I guide her back to the sidewalk where Vivian is waiting. "Let's head inside."

—

"What kiss?" Hudson frowns down at the tablet, "Who did you kiss?"

Vivian's mouth pops open, "You."

"Did you?" Hudson frowns but I see the lie as clear as day on his face. He didn't want to admit it. "I don't remember that."

What. An. Asshole. I'll call it how it is.

"Oh," Vivian chews her lip, "Okay then."

I shake my head at him. I haven't known these girls for long, but they'd somehow become important to me. I made it a point not to get attached to my charges, it was only a job after all but I had. First to Ray and then to the others. Vivian deserved better than that.

Hudson was quick to threaten me, which is laughable, about Ray, but he's hurting Vivian blatantly.

"So, what do we do now?" Hudson leans back in his chair, his eyes barely brushing Vivian and looks to me.

"Call the cops, let them know we received another email and send it across."

Hudson nods, "You got somewhere else to stay tonight?" He asks Vivian without actually looking at her.

My bets are he has a thing for the model, probably always has but hates to admit it. This is a man who takes his work very seriously and getting involved with one of his girls will look bad for business.

Hell, I got it. Getting involved with Ray wasn't exactly professional but fuck that. I didn't care.

"You can stay with me," he picks up his phone, letting the words hang between them.

"No," Vivian says abruptly, "I'll stay with Ray."

Ray's been watching them back and forth and then she nods, "That's fine."

There go my plans to take her out tonight. I push down my disappointment.

I just want to get her alone. All to myself.

I listen whilst Hudson speaks to the officer assigned to the case and when he puts the phone down I tell the girls to head downstairs and I'll meet them there. When we're finally alone I spin on him, "That was a dick move."

"Excuse me?"

"You fucking remember kissing her and you're pretending you didn't, why?"

"I have no idea what you're talking about," he growls, "I'm also not paying you to get involved in my shit."

"No, you're paying me to protect the girl you just fucking squashed. That was a low blow, dude."

A flicker of emotion crosses his face but then he schools his features and settles back, "Is that all?"

"I never put you down as being an asshole, Hud. That's just fucking disappointing."

"Now that you've had your two cents," He barks, "Get the hell out of my office."

"Gladly," I snap and storm to the door, "Oh, and just

remember, she's going through this too. This isn't easy on her, knowing there's a creep *stalking* her. She could probably use a friend right now."

He doesn't respond so I take my exit, heading down to the lobby. I spot Ray first, she's a beacon for my eyes, all that glossy dark hair and her tight little body calling out to me. My blood heats at the mere sight of her.

I haven't been able to get the image of her under me from my head but the picture of her straddled over my hips, riding my cock, now that was burned into my brain.

Twenty-three

Ray

I watch as Vivian disappears into her building to collect her belongings and when she's out of sight I turn on Zach.

"What are you hiding?"

Because I know he is hiding something. He was acting weird in the car and I am one hundred percent certain there were no road works. We drive that road every day and the city doesn't just forget to signpost it.

Instead of answering my question he steps into me, pinning me up against the side of the car and caging me in between his arms.

His mouth drops to mine, his tongue sweeping through my lips.

My brain short circuits. Literally. Suddenly all I think and see and smell, is him.

"I've wanted to do that since I saw you this morning," he growls against my mouth, "God you make me crazy."

 Instead of coherent words leaving my lips I just whimper as his hands squeeze my waist and he presses his body into me, grinding his growing erection into my lower abdomen. My hands fist his hair, holding him to me.

 What was I talking about again? Fuck if I know.

 "Real shame you're busy tonight," he mumbles, "I had other plans for you."

 To prove his point, he nudges my legs open with his knee and then dips his hips, seeming to find the right spot to grind against to leave me a whimpering wet mess. The fact that we are very clearly in public and everyone can see what the hell is going on, I should really try to put a stop to this but clearly my body hasn't caught up as my hands tug his shirt from his pants and I run my nails over the ladder of his abs, feeling every dip and ridge.

 He eventually pulls from the kiss but doesn't move far, he simply rests his forehead against mine. His eyes are the colour of liquid silver, lids hooded as his tongue sweeps across his lips.

 "You have no idea how much I want you right now."

 "Mm," I agree, leaning in to whisper my lips against his.

 "But the next time I have you, it will be *after* I've wined and dined you."

 A burst of laughter escapes my throat, "That's awfully presumptuous of you."

 "You saying you don't want it," he teases, pressing his hips into me. Gah! Pleasure erupts between my legs as the friction of him rubs against my clit.

 "That's what I thought," he chuckles lightly.

"Right I'm ready!" Vivian calls as she steps back out of the building.

We jump apart but I mean who are we kidding? Zach's practically undressed, his shirt wrinkled from my hands and his hair dishevelled and I have no doubt I look similar.

Her eyes bounce between us and then a knowing smile curls her lips, "I knew it!"

Deny. Deny. Deny.

"Zach was just, uh, he was just," I have nothing. Zach smirks and tucks himself in before striding over to Vivian and picking up her bag.

Vivian skips over to me, "You're totally screwing him! When did this happen!?"

"Get in the damn car," I grumble.

"You don't have to tell me right now, but later. With wine. And chips!" She squeals.

I feel his eyes on me as we drive towards my apartment but I can't bring myself to look. I know what I'll see there. Desire. Longing. *Heat.* And with the way I'm currently burning I have no idea how I'll stop myself from climbing through the seats to straddle his lap.

Zach is the type of man your mama warns you about. The type that gets under your skin, makes you feel so Goddamn good. The type of man who *ruins* you for anyone else.

He has the power to both lift you up and crush you in the same breath.

And that thought alone is terrifying.

He looks at me as if he wants to devour me whole, leaving nothing left.

I chance a glance in his direction and his eyes crinkle at the sides when our eyes meet.

It's so freaking hot in this car it's stifling. I push the button to let down the window and all but hang out of it like a dog.

I make him crazy?

He has absolutely no idea what he does to me.

How does he manage to push all other thoughts away? How does he make me feel safe with his presence alone? The email before, that had my insides churning like a washing machine but then he took control of the situation and all that worry just disappeared.

I liked to be strong. I liked to be independent but even I can't deny that I *need* Zach.

How did that even happen?

I let the man into my bed – well his bed actually – and he now owns me.

Turns out, I don't hate it.

—

"Tell me everything," Vivian sits with her legs crossed, a glass of wine cupped in her hand and her grin mischievous whilst Harper hangs over the edge of the sofa, listening eagerly. Oli saunters back in from the kitchen with a beer.

After I turned up with Vivian, Harper made it her mission to turn tonight into a girl's night. And after Vivian 'let slip' that something was going on with Zach and I, they were all suddenly very eager to get round here with wine and snacks.

Oli throws herself down onto the chair by the window and tips her beer to her lips. "Go on."

"There's nothing to tell," I lie, scooping up some dip onto a chip and plopping it into my mouth.

"I smell bullshit!" Oli yells.

I glower at her.

"Come on," Vivian knocks my knee, "Why don't you want to tell us?"

"Really, there isn't anything to tell. We slept together," I shrug, "And he wants to take me out."

"When did this happen?" Harper asks.

"Saturday," I say in a small voice.

Harper gasps, "You said you were at the library!"

"Well," I drag the word out, "I lied. I'm sorry!"

"You are not forgiven," Harper pouts, crossing her arms. I know she's not serous but still, I hate that I lied.

"This isn't what we should be talking about anyway," I tell them, "What about that email?"

They all shrug, "What about it?"

"How are you all so cool about this?"

"If we worry, he has power and why would we want to give him that? He's all mouth anyway."

I cock a brow, "Uh, my car says differently."

Vivian winces, "I know but what more can he do? He's too afraid to actually get out from behind his computer so he's lowered himself to harassment and vandalism. The cops will catch him."

"I don't like that we have no idea who it is." I say. Was I the only one actually taking this seriously?

"Me either," Harper agrees.

"Ray," Oli leans forward, "He's not going to do anything. You and Vivi have Zach and neither Harper or me have had anything happen. I doubt he even realises we exist. The only reason you were targeted is because you two are always together."

I nod. That made sense.

"Maybe you're right."

"I'm always right," Oli grins, "Now drink your wine and *please* tell me what Zach is like in bed? He looks like he'd be amazing."

I roll my eyes, "He really was."

"And he wants to take you out? To like dinner?"

I sip my wine and nod my head, a swarm of butterflies erupting in my stomach. I had asked him out first, sure I had said it wasn't a date, but it was even if I wouldn't admit it at the time.

By the time the girls finally had enough of Zach talk, they were all way past drunk whilst I was still completely sober, and my mind was consumed.

This was going to be a long night.

Twenty-four

Zach

"Are you sure you sent me the right thing?" The voice on the line grumbles.

"Yes, I'm sure," I bark, "did *you* mix it up with something else?"

"This is a well-established lab, Mr Wyatt, as you well know."

I run a hand through my hair.

"Are you sure the results are correct?"

He sighs, "Yes, I ran it three times."

Turns out, the powder residue on the glass. Well it was dishwasher granules. Fucking dishwasher granules. I'm losing my damn mind!

"Okay," I sigh because I have nothing else to say, "Thanks."

I couldn't fault the lab. He got me the results quicker than I expected, granted it wasn't what I was expecting.

Clearly my own paranoia was getting the best of me. I should be happy with this, but I can't shake the feeling that I am missing something. It's been eating at me for a few days. I have re-read those emails, looking for clues, I've replayed each scene in my head a hundred times and yet there's this black spot right in the middle and no matter what angle I look at it, nothing is giving it away.

I knew this was far from over. The email today clarified that.

After I hang up, I call my brother. It's been a while since I spoke to him and I wanted to speak to my niece. Family was everything to me.

"Hey bro," his familiar voice crackles down the line, "How's LA life?"

I think about Ray. Despite the fucked up situation, at least I had something good, "Good man, how are you?"

"Yeah fine," he sounds tired.

"What's going on?" I sit up straighter, watching the screen of my computer go dark as it shuts itself off to sleep.

"I didn't want to tell you over the phone, you're still coming in a few weeks right?"

My vacation had been planned for weeks now, I hadn't told anyone about it yet but I had cover sorted already, "Yes. But tell me now? What's going on?"

Scott sighs, "Dad's not been so hot lately. Chest pains. Fatigue. He's been in and out of the hospital getting tests."

"What the fuck!" I bellow, "And I'm only finding out about this now?"

"Zach, chill, it's fine. He's dealing with it and you know I'd tell you if anything serious was going on."

"This is serious."

My dad wasn't exactly a spring chicken anymore. Chest pains and other symptoms weren't exactly a good sign.

"Zach, it's fine. This is why I wasn't going to tell you yet."

This day just kept getting better and better. We talk for a little longer but then my frustrations get the better of me and I hang up. Before I even realise what I'm doing I'm pulling up Ray's contact information.

What are you doing?

Reading. The girls are all passed out.

My keys are in my hand, along with my helmet and leather jacket. The air tonight is cool, the sky covered in a thick layer of clouds. The silver of the moon creates this halo effect through the blanket. I throw a leg over the seat and turn the key.

If you could be doing anything right now, what would it be? I ask before pulling the helmet over my head and setting off onto the road. I feel the buzz of my phone in my pocket, telling me of her reply but I can't look. It doesn't take long before my bike is rolling to a stop outside of the building.

Truth?

Truth. I reply.

I'd have liked to go on that date tonight.

I grin like a teenage boy.

Come downstairs.

Why?

Just do as you're told.

Anyone ever tell you you're really bossy? Maybe I don't want to.

I press the call button.

"Hello?"

"Get your fine ass in that elevator and come downstairs," I growl.

"Are you here?"

"Sweetheart, my patience will only go so far."

She giggles, "And what if I don't?"

"Then I'm going to come to your apartment, kick your door down and carry you off like the mad man I am."

She full on laughs, "Maybe I'd like that."

Her husky voice goes straight to my dick, "Don't tease me sweetheart. Come down."

"Let me get dressed first," she says. I hear the rustle of her moving around and then a door close.

"Wait," I practically yell.

"What?"

"What are you wearing?"

"I'm sure you'd like me to tell you that we're all sat around in tank tops and panties, eating ice cream and having pillow fights."

That's more West's thing, "I mean that does paint a pretty picture," I say, "But tell me."

"I'm in a pair of pyjama pants and an old Uni sweater."

"Sexy," I grin. Knowing Ray it *was* sexy. Everything she wore was sexy.

"Don't I know it," she laughs, "I'm putting the phone down now. I'll be down in a minute."

"Don't make me wait, Ray." I warn before she hangs up.

I lean back on the bike, crossing my arms as I watch through the glass doors for her to arrive. The street is quiet, a few dogs bark and there's a rustling behind some dumpsters near by but in this late hour it feels like I'm the only one awake.

The elevator doors open, and she steps out. My heart

damn near skips a beat.

Is that fucking normal?

Her longs legs are clad in denim, the material ripped all the way up and she has on a tight white tank top with a grey cardigan thrown over the top.

Her cheeks warm as she steps out into the cooler air and she darts a look up and down the sidewalk before her eyes finally meet mine.

"Come here," I grumble, reaching an arm out for her.

She doesn't hesitate. She steps right up into them and for the first time since I left her here a few hours ago do I settle. I press my lips into her glossy hair and close my eyes as her heat washes over me. Her arms wrap around my middle and she presses her face into my chest.

"Is it strange that I missed you?" I ask. It wasn't a question I meant to say out loud but there we go.

She tilts her chin up to look at me and then shakes her head, a small smile playing over her lips. "No. I missed you too."

I lean in and kiss her, telling myself not to get carried away and then grin, "Hop on."

"The bike or…?"

Holy shit. *This woman.*

"The bike," I growl.

"You just had to say so," she flutters her lashes innocently and then steps from my embrace, accepting the helmet I hand out to her. I shrug out of my jacket too.

"Put this on."

She cocks her brow, "It's going to be huge."

"Yeah, so?"

She rolls her eyes and tugs the jacket on, her arms not even making it to the ends. I zip it up all the way and nod my head, "Perfect."

"Mm-hmm." She grumbles, kicking her leg over the bike. Her arms wrap around my middle as her thighs squeeze me. I don't actually have a plan, I just wanted to see her so I go the one place that calms me.

It had been a few days since I had managed to get down to the beach and I loved to swim. The easiest option is the pool back at the condo but there's nothing quite like the ocean. Not that we would be swimming tonight.

I park the bike in front of the sand and help Ray off, tugging the helmet from her head. She smooths down her hair and stares out to the dark waves crashing against the shore. It's so dark, with the moon shrouded in clouds you can barely make out the waves, but you can certainly hear them.

"I love coming down here," She murmurs, "Nighttime especially. It's almost a different place when no one is around."

"I agree," I step up behind her, wrapping my arms around her shoulders and bringing her into me as I sit back onto the bike. She follows, perching in my lap.

We sit in silence for a while, listening to the waves crashing against the sand. The city is so large and so busy, you almost forget to take a moment to breathe. You forget that you can find peace in a sea of chaos and now, with Ray in my arms, I feel so at ease it actually scares me how quickly everything has become so natural.

I could see myself falling in love with the woman. Hell, I might already be halfway there. The thought alone should terrify me, but I find it doesn't. Not even a little.

I pull her in closer, sealing any space between our bodies until I can no longer find where I stop and she begins.

A contented sigh leaves her lips, "How did this happen?" She murmurs.

"What's that sweetheart?"

"Well last week I wanted to strangle you," she giggles.

"At the same time as wanting to ride me," I growl in her ear, nipping her lobe with my teeth.

She responds by grinding her ass into my lap. My dick certainly liked it.

"Maybe."

"Mm," I grumble, "Love and war go hand in hand."

"Perhaps they do," She agrees.

"I'd like to war a little more."

"What?" She looks at me over her shoulder, her brows puckering.

"Make up sex is always the best, my second favourite is angry sex."

"There's something wrong with you," she shakes her head.

"No sweetheart," I kiss her temple, "There's something *right* with you."

Twenty-five

Ray

"Where are we going?" I ask, climbing back onto the bike and wrapping my arms around his middle.

"Dinner."

"Uh, I hate to break it to you," I tell him, "It's three in the morning."

"Breakfast?"

I don't argue. Truth be told I don't want this night to be over. Sitting down at the beach with him was so peaceful. The silence was companionable, his arms wrapped around me like it's where they belonged. He drives the empty roads of the city and then stops at a diner that's actually still open. It's retro themed with black and white tiled floors and fifties styled booths covered in shiny PVC and framed pictures of Elvis on the walls. The scent of coffee and pancakes hits me as we walk in the door.

There's another couple in the restaurant, looking tired and little drunk but that's it.

We find a booth near the back before a waitress in a blue dress and white apron saunters over.

"What can I get you?" Despite the early hour she's spritely.

"Coffee," I say, "And the pancakes."

"I'll have what she's having," Zach tells her. She scribbles across the pad and disappears. "It's not what I had in mind," Zach continues once we're alone.

"It's perfect," I tell him.

He grins, a real boyish grin that does funny things to my insides. Who knew the caveman had a soft side too?

He bumps my foot under the table, "I assume all has been quiet tonight?"

"No emails," I tell him.

"Good."

"Do you have any idea what's actually happening?"

He shakes his head, "And I hate it. I don't like not knowing."

"The girls are all so casual about it, Vivian doesn't even seem worried."

He purses his lips, "She should be."

I pull my lip between my teeth, "The cops have nothing."

"Let's not talk about this," Zach reaches over and squeezes my hand, "I don't want to ruin this."

We drink our coffee and eat our pancakes to lighter topics but the thoughts aren't far from my mind. We'll still have to deal with them tomorrow and the next day and the next, until this guy is caught. I can deal with my car being smashed up. I can't deal with the people

I love getting hurt in the process.

After we're done, we hang about in the diner until my lids start to get heavy. Tomorrow – *today* will be tough on no sleep but do I regret it? Not a chance. Zach takes me back to my apartment and I slide the helmet from my head and shrug out of his leather jacket. "Come upstairs."

"Is that good idea?" He smirks.

"Always."

His eyes darken and he stands, following me through the doors and to the elevator. When inside the metal cart, he pins me to the wall and kisses me like I'm his last breath. I can taste the coffee and syrup on his tongue. He barely lets me go as we step onto my floor and down the hall to the door.

"You need to be quiet," I tell him, pulling away from his mouth, "They're sleeping in the living room."

I unlock the door and push it open a touch, peering inside. Silence and darkness greets me so I drag Zach in behind me, closing the door with a quiet click and bolting it. If I go to bed now, I'll be able to get an hour or two in before I have to get up for the day. I tiptoe further into the apartment, my eyes landing on the three sleeping bodies sprawled in the lounge. Harper is on the couch, Vivian curled up on a makeshift bed made from cushions on the floor and Oli is curled into a fetal position on the chair. Zach follows my gaze and cocks a brow.

"Is this normal for you girls?" He whispers.

I cock my head from side to side, thinking about it, "Pretty much."

If I hadn't gone out with Zach tonight, I'd be right there with them, probably curled up on the couch with Harper, likely using her thigh as a pillow. I drag him down the hall and open my bedroom door, ushering him inside.

I switch on the lamp by the bedside and then head to the closest, stripping out of my clothes. I'm halfway undressed when I feel his eyes on me.

"Ray," he groans like he's in pain.

My eyes widen a fraction, "What is it?"

"Baby," he crosses the space between us, stopping my hands from pushing down my jeans. He's seen me naked before. What's the problem? "If you want to sleep, you're gonna need to stop."

I frown, "What?"

"I can't deal with you naked. I can't think straight with all this skin on show."

"Is that right?"

A little devious smile pulls on my mouth as I push his hands away and push the jeans down my thighs. He follows them, his eyes darkening with every inch of skin exposed. His tongue wets his bottom lip, a muscle in his jaw ticks and his hands flex at his sides. I push them all the way down and slip them off my feet, letting them drop to the floor. I'm left in just my bra and panties, non-matching but Zach doesn't seem to mind. I reach behind and unclasp my bra, letting the material fall down my arms and away from my body and then move to my knickers, sliding them down my legs until I'm left fully exposed to him.

I should feel vulnerable, being so naked when he's fully clothed but all I feel is empowered, especially with the way his eyes devour me, taking in every inch of my body, from my shoulders to my toes.

He cups a hand over his mouth as I step backwards towards my bed. When my knees hit the foot I drop down and shimmy my way up until I'm resting on the pillows, never once do my eyes stray from him.

"Sweetheart," he groans, following me, his steps haggard, "You need to put some clothes on."

"I don't want to."

His eyes flick to my face and then suddenly, he's stripping out of his jeans and tee, throwing them to the floor behind him. He grabs my ankles and pulls me down the bed, stopping when I'm beneath him

"You are so fucking beautiful," he grumbles kissing my jaw.

He kisses down my throat, over my collar bone and down to my breast, sucking a nipple into his mouth. My back arches into him, my core throbbing with the need to be filled by him.

His fingers tickle up my inner thigh and then he finds the sweet spot that's already so wet for him I should be embarrassed, but with the way he groans as his fingers work me up can only make me feel fucking superhuman. He works me into a frenzy with his fingers, pushing me to the crest only to stop when I'm on the brink.

"I swear to God, Zach," I growl at him.

"Does my girl need release?" He teases.

"*Your* girl?"

"Damn fucking straight, *my* girl," He pushes a finger inside, hooking it as he sweeps across my G spot whilst his thumb presses into my nub, "This is mine. Mine to kiss, and touch and fuck."

"Presumptuous," I breathe.

"I only tell the truth," he tells me against my mouth, flicking his tongue inside but not actually kissing me.

My hips grind against his hand, "Zach."

"Do you want my cock, sweetheart?"

"Yes!"

"Condom?"

"Nightstand."

He reaches over, forces the drawer open and rips the foil open with his teeth. "Put it on."

I don't need to be asked twice. I take the condom from him, grip his shaft and roll it on, squeezing my fingers around his cock until his eyes roll back and his lips part. I work him over the condom, pushing my hand up and down, and reaching out with my other hand to cup his balls.

"Fuck," he hisses between his teeth.

He suddenly pins me to the bed, forces my legs open and enters me in one swift movement. We moan in unison.

"I'm not going to be gentle," he warns.

"Good," I snap back.

His eyes darken even further as he grabs me from behind my knees and forces my legs up, placing them on both his shoulders as he shifts to settle on his knees. His hands wrap around the tops of my thighs and then he begins to slam into me, again and again, and again. Our skin slaps together and I grab a pillow to shove over my face to stifle my moans. His fingers grip in a biting hold, his hips pounding into me relentlessly.

"Fuck, Ray," he moans in ecstasy, "You feel so good. So fucking good."

Suddenly he flips me, grips my hips and brings my ass up, keeping my shoulders pinned to the bed. He enters me again from behind, his hands holding me around the waist. He's able to go deeper in this position, angling his hips until I swear I can feel him so far inside me it doesn't feel real.

"Oh god," I moan, my voice muffled by my sheets.

"That's right sweetheart."

He kneads my ass and I can feel my release building.

This intense burn that clenches around my muscles and zips down my spine.

"I'm going to come," I cry out, meeting him thrust for thrust.

"Yes," he growls

He reaches around to toy with my clit, never once wavering from his punishing rhythm.

My orgasm grips me, sending me over the edge until I see stars blurring my vision.

"Oh God, I feel you," he grits out, "I feel you clenching around my cock."

He keeps the pleasure going, riding out my orgasm until I can feel him swelling inside me. His pulse becomes erratic and then he shouts out his own release, collapsing down on my back.

Our sweat slicked skin slides against one another's as our breathing comes out in short, raspy breaths.

If sex with Zach will always be like this, then sign me up for a life time.

Twenty-six

Ray

Why is it so fucking hot? My hair is stuck to my forehead, my back is wet with sweat and Jesus Christ why does it feel like there is a bear pinning me to the bed.

I force my eyes open, groggy as hell from lack of sleep and reach out to pull off whatever it is clinging to me. My hands find solid muscle and smooth skin. Zach.

He's got one arm thrown over my chest and his leg tucked around both of mine whilst his face is buried into the crook of my neck. A small amount of light is streaming in through the crack in the curtain and subtly I turn my head to look him over. His bare muscular back is on show, only a slither of the sheet covering his ass, but his thighs are on show, his feet

173

dangling off the end of the bed. He's on his front and I can't see his face, but this view is just as good. I can almost make out every muscle, every curve and dip of his back like he's been carved from stone. Before him, I didn't believe men like him existed but here we are.

Despite the fantastic view and the hunk of a male clinging to me like a monkey, I can't breathe in this heat. I begin to fidget, as softly as I can and as my muscles twinge, memories of last night swim to the surface. My core tightens but there's no time right now. I can hear the girls moving around in the front room, their voices filtering in from beneath the door and knowing them, it won't be long before they force their way in here. They're going to get the shock of their lives if they do.

I manage to pry his arm from my chest, tucking it down the side of his body but his legs are turning out to be quite the problem. With my torso free, I sit up and hook my hands under his thigh, trying to lift it. It's like lifting a tree.

"Where are you sneaking off to?" His deep, sleepy voice rumbles against the pillow.

"It's late," I tell him in a whisper.

"Or early," he grumbles, "What time is it?"

I flick my eyes to the clock on the bedside, "Just after seven."

I have not slept nearly enough and if I could get away with it, I would sleep all day but duty calls.

Zach has other ideas.

All that hard work to get him off of me has gone to waste as he tugs me back down to the bed, covering my body with his.

His grey eyes twinkle as he looks me over, his fingers brushing my hair from my forehead, "Good morning, sunshine."

"Sunshine?" I muse.

"Mm, you're a *Ray* of sunshine."

I roll my eyes, "Get off me, I have to get ready."

He grinds his hips forward, pushing his already hard cock into my sex, "Let me help."

I giggle, "This isn't helping. If we're not careful, the girls are going to get quite the show."

"Let them watch," he kisses me, my lips, my nose, my cheeks. Before long, he's working me back up, turning my insides to liquid and my blood to fire. I groan as his lips close around a nipple but then a heavy knock sounds on the door.

"Are you decent?" Harper's voice shouts through the door, "I'm coming in."

"No!" I screech. "Uh, I mean, I'm not decent. I'm very, very naked."

"Oh, okay," Harper says, "I've made coffee."

"Okay!"

Zach laughs deep, his nose running down my throat.

"Get off me!" I order but it's one of those things that has absolutely no conviction, especially as my own hips grind against him, sliding my core up and down his shaft. I swear my body has a mind of its own. Traitor.

"One condition," he licks my bottom lip.

"Oh, blackmail now."

"Sweetheart," he deadpans, "I will use any means necessary to keep you under me."

Do. Not. Give. In.

"Name your terms."

He grins, "Stay with me tonight. At my place."

"So you can have your way with me some more?"

"That and so I can actually cook for you. So we can sit on my couch and watch a movie. So I can take you

Victoria McFarlane

to my bed and sleep with you in my arms all night, not just a few hours."

I turn to mush, "Deal."

One chaste kiss later, he's climbing off me, his naked body stepping from the bed. I could look at him all day, all of him in naked glory and *it is glorious.* He finds his jeans and tugs them over his legs before snapping up his t shirt. Finally, I climb out too, heading to the closet to pull on my house coat so I can head straight for the shower.

"I'll be back in an hour to collect you and Vivian," he tells me, stepping up to me. His fingertips feather down the side of my face before cupping my jaw and tilting me to kiss him.

I have no idea how to explain his appearance in the apartment not that I'm really going to need too. The girls aren't stupid, they can add two and two together.

I follow him from the room, down the hall and into the living room.

Everything stops, all goes silent, I'm pretty sure even the clock on the wall stops ticking as each one of my friends turns to look at us. Their mouths hang open, their eyes wide.

"Morning ladies," Zach rumbles as he heads to the door.

I pluck up the coffee from the side and once the door closes behind him, I try to make a run for it, my eyes trained on the bathroom door. Just a few more feet and I can hold off on the questions for at least another fifteen minutes.

"Ah ah ah!" Oli jumps in front of me, guarding the door and I feel the other two step up behind me. What is this?

"I kinda need a shower guys," I shrug, sipping my coffee, "And to get ready. Busy day today. Busy.

Busy. Busy."

"Why was Zach here?" She ignores me. "More importantly, what are you wearing under your robe?"

"Nothing." I shrug.

They already know I'm sleeping with him, why are they making this such a big deal.

"How did you even sneak him in here?"

"You were all knocked out, it was pretty easy actually."

"Is that a hickey!?" Oli tugs the collar of my robe down.

My cheeks flush crimson, "Come on, can I just shower now please? We really don't need to discuss this."

"Like fuck we don't, you're getting some and none of us are, we need details."

I roll my eyes, "Stop with the dramatics, you've had the details."

Finally they leave me alone and I step into the bathroom, dropping the robe to the floor whilst still sipping at the coffee. If I could just have a constant drip of caffeine, that would be grand. I look at my naked self in the mirror, noting the slight redness to my skin where Zach's scruff has scraped at me and the marks on my neck from his mouth but the thing I notice the most, I am glowing. I feel amazing. I feel wanted and needed and em-fucking-powered.

The water doesn't wash away the feeling. I still sense his hands on my body, his lips on mine, his voice inside my head. I'm sure it shouldn't feel like this, but I can't find it in me to care. I should be worried. He's a man I could fall for. Quickly too. The way he makes me feel. It's everything all rolled into one, like I'm going to combust at any given time and declare it all.

When I'm dried and dressed, I pull on a flowing yellow dress, tucked in around the waist and my beige sandals, leaving my hair wet as I braid it and let it fall down over one shoulder. Oli has left already, probably heading to the shelter and Vivian is lounging over the couch, her nose in her phone whilst Harper makes another pot of coffee.

I've managed to hide the dark circles under my eyes with concealer, but it doesn't help how tired I actually feel. I'm running on about an hours' worth of sleep. A lot of caffeine is going to be needed to get through the day.

It's been exactly one hour when the buzzer for the door sounds.

I grab my travel mug of coffee and head down with Vivian, my stomach erupting into a swarm of butterflies even though I saw him not so long ago. When I step from the doors, he's leaning casually against the door, dressed in his signature black slacks and white button down, looking as fresh as ever. You would never believe the man was running on only a few hours of sleep. His eyes are lively, his posture strong and capable whereas I look more haggard and clumsy.

He smiles at Vivian as he opens the door and she climbs in but before I can, he curls his hand around my wrist and tugs me to his body. Unable to stop myself I bounce into his chest and his lips descend, his tongue sweeping in to tangle with mine.

"Good morning, Ray," he grins.

"You said that already." I touch my fingers to my lips. There was something different about that kiss.

"Did I?"

"Mm-hmm," I cock a brow.

"Bad memory," he tsks.

178

"Mm-hmm."

"So much sass," he licks his lips.

"You're going to tell me that turns you on, aren't you?"

"Like you have no idea."

Twenty-seven

Zach

I needed to get a grip and do my fucking job.

Watch Vivian. Make sure she's safe. Keep the weirdos at bay.

Not watch Ray flitter around in that little yellow dress, picturing what it would look like to wrap that braid around my fist and take her from behind.

God, all I've been doing today is thinking through my cock. Thankfully, Vivian's been hulled up in a studio, leaving me to stand on the outskirts with Ray but between her scent and her tight little body I have barely any room to think about anything else.

I run a hand up her bare arm and lean in to kiss her ear, watching the way her body quakes with a shiver and her lashes flutter closed.

I've been with plenty of women. I've had long term and short term girlfriends but none of them have ever made me feel like this. They've never made this light appear inside me or made me feel like I'm ten feet fucking tall.

The way she looks at me, the way she kisses me, I want to parade around like a peacock, I want to puff out and pound on my chest and tell the fucking world she's *my* girl. Mine. No one elses. She looks at me like I've just hung the moon and the stars and if that doesn't make me feel like I could conquer the world then I don't know what would.

"People are staring," Ray mumbles as my lips trail along her jaw.

"Let them stare."

"They're going to think us highly unprofessional," she breathes as my teeth snag her ear lobe. Is there a closet around here I could haul her off too? I'm sure I could find one.

"Let them think," I reply, my tongue tasting her skin.

"Zach," she pleads.

"You want me to stop sweetheart?"

Her head shakes no but her mouth answers, "Yes."

"That's some mixed signals right there."

"Gah," she presses her hands to her cheeks when I straighten back up and tuck my hands behind my back, taking the at ease position like I hadn't just been fondling my charges assistant. Truthfully, there's so much I can do to her without anyone even so much as batting an eye, but I won't push her. All those things, the risk and the adrenaline, that can wait for another day.

"You still coming tonight?" I grin at my use of words.

Her eyes narrow in on my face, "Yes, we had a deal."
"Is that all it was?" I cock a brow, "A deal."
"Damn straight," she squares her shoulders, "Now if you'll excuse me, I need coffee."

I watch her walk away, my eyes following the lines of her body. This woman had brought me to my knees. Figuratively. I had no doubt she would bring me down literally too.

I hadn't expected this when I first met her in that bar. Hell, I hadn't expected it when I riled her up the second time we met. The heat between us, the intense chemistry, I put it down to attraction. Simple. But this was more than that.

Ray was a stunning woman. Both inside and out. She cares deeply, is fiercely loyal and has a heart so pure she shouldn't even be looking at a guy like me twice.

I'm selfish though, so like hell would I ever point that out. I wasn't a bad guy, but I was no stranger to violence. I've seen my share of horror, like nothing she could ever imagine.

My phone buzzes in my pocket and I pull it out, seeing Scott's name flashing across the screen.

"Hey bro," I follow her body until I can't see her anymore and then lean back on the wall, facing forward again.

"Zach," he greets, "You care to fill me in on your current assignment?"

"My current assignment involves following around a model." I play it down, "Nothing to fill in."

If I had actually told Scott about the details of the job, he'd be demanding I set a second person on the case and filter everything through him. I loved my brother, truly I did, but I didn't want him in on this. This was my first case since opening the new office and he'd controlled everything up until now. And I didn't want a second person, I didn't need it, I had everything under control.

"So why did the lab call me telling me you handed in a specimen you believed contained Rohypnol?"

"How did you find out about that?" I grumble. That lab was supposed to keep a god damn secret. They had been used for years so why now are they tattling to my brother.

"The guy you used, he's been a friend of mine, long before you, he tells me everything to do with *our* business."

I grit my teeth, "It was a theory. Nothing for you to worry about."

"Is there something going on that I should know about?"

"No," I growl, "Now if you're quite finished questioning my capabilities, I have shit to do."

"Wait, Zach," his voice stops me from hitting the red button on the screen. "Sorry, I didn't mean to upset you."

"You pissed me off," I clarify.

"Yes, same thing," He sighs, "We're a team. You should come to me if you need help."

"I don't need help, Scott," I snap back. "If I did, I would have called."

"No, your pride and pig-headedness would have seen you didn't. Look, please just call if you want any help from me, I don't know the ins and outs of the assignment but if you're requesting results because you think you're charge has been roofied, you need to let me know. There's paperwork we need to complete."

I think of the mountain of paperwork stacked on my desk back at the condo. Yeah right there was shit ton to fill out and whilst I had done it, I hadn't submitted it. With each new email I should report it back, shit, I should have reported when Ray's car was smashed to pieces, but I didn't. Why?

Pride.

It was a fickle beast.

I knew it was wrong and yet I couldn't bring myself to ask for help.

Having my brother look at it might actually mean that black spot I can sense but not see might actually get filled out with a fresh pair of eyes but still, my lips don't utter the words they should and I stay silent.

"Turns out it was dishwasher granules, perhaps I've just become paranoid like my big bother," I joke.

He grunts, "There would be a reason for it. You're a smart man, Zachary," he uses my full name the same way my father would, "Your intuition speaks volumes."

"I've got to go, Scott," I pinch the bridge of my nose and sigh, "my *charge* requires my assistance."

My phone vibrates in my hand but I don't bring it away to check the messages.

"Don't be an idiot about this," Scott chides, "Speak soon."

I hang up without another word and then bring up the text message I had gotten whilst on the call.

It's from an unknown number, one that is hidden but I'm sure I could get the tech guys to unearth it.

You have her now. It won't last long.

I frown down at the message. It's obvious who it's from but it's the first time the message hasn't been directed at Vivian via Ray and the email account she manages. I wasn't sure how the guy could be confused about my status with the model, it was obvious I was her hired bodyguard and nothing I had done would suggest otherwise. Unless that's not what he is referring too.

Perhaps he was referring to her being under my protection and how that wouldn't last long. If it was a veiled threat, it was a shoddy one at best.

Scoffing I close down the texting app and pocket my phone.

If he thought he could intimidate me, he had another thing coming.

Ray turns the corner, holding two mugs of steaming coffee and beams at me when she meets my eyes.

The call and text forgotten, I smile back.

There's no reason to share the text or the phone call and I take the offered mug, sipping at the liquid. Just how I like it.

"How did you know?" I ask.

She shrugs, "Just a guess."

Black with one sugar.

We stand side by side for the rest of the day, her arm pressed up against me. I'm sure it's meant it to be platonic, but with the way her skin ignites against mine, it was anything but.

Twenty-eight

Ray

Zach drops Vivian and me back at my apartment just after six that evening with the promise to pick me up at eight.

"You two are serious," Vivian comments as I unlock my apartment door and head to the kitchen to prepare dinner.

I shrug, "I don't know what we are."

Harper wasn't home yet which was surprising. She was usually home before I was, tucked up on the couch with either a book or the TV. I fire over a text to make sure she's okay before pulling out all the ingredients from the fridge to make a carbonara for Vivian and her. I would be eating with Zach later, so I was going to save myself.

Fine. Harper texts back, *The renovations today have hit a bit of a snag so I'm just clearing up some mess. See you later.*

I send her a kissy face back. She'll be able to heat her dinner in the microwave later.

Vivian settles on the couch. It was decided she'd spend the next few days here. Whilst her apartment was airtight, we wanted to make sure she would be safe, and nothing says safety more than numbers. A little bit of guilt ate at me over the fact that I would be heading to Zach's tonight, but she wouldn't be alone. Harper and her were just as close. The four of us, Me, Harper, Oli and Vivian, we were sisters. The girl group everyone dreamed to have as friends. There was never any bitchiness, no nastiness, we were friends through and through and I don't think there was anything that could change that.

It was nice to have a best friend for a boss. My job never actually felt like a job at all.

I set the pasta onto boil and fry up some bacon and mushrooms, pouring myself and Vivian a glass of white wine.

Old fashioned was my choice of drink on a night out most of the time but I could never make them the same way at home, it was really quite a simple cocktail but they always tasted better when someone else made them. Vivian takes a healthy sip and smiles at me over the rim.

"What?" I demand.

"You're *glowing*," She giggles.

"I am not."

"Are to!" She settles her wine into her lap, "It's not a bad thing, Ray, I'm happy he makes you happy."

I chew on the inside of my lip, a nagging thought tugging at my mind, "You're not mad?"

"Why an earth would I be mad!?"

"Well he's *your* bodyguard and I'm your assistant?"

"Let's get one thing straight," her eyes bore into mine, "You'll never just be my assistant, you're my friend and yes he is my bodyguard and I like him. He's a nice guy." I scoff. He wasn't a nice guy. He was an asshole. Who somehow managed to get under my skin *and* in my panties.

I no longer thought of him as an asshole though. That was a mask he wore, one he donned well, now he was the sweet talker who stole my breath every time he was near.

"You two look good together," she continues, "He's like every alpha male you read in those books you love."

"That you love too!" I defend.

She nods her head and tips her wine glass to me, "True"

He really was the alpha male that you fall in love with though. All surly and masculine and with his looks, I wouldn't be surprised if I ever saw him posed as a cover model on one of those said books. It wasn't just his looks though, granted he was *godly,* but he had this soft underbelly that just begged to be explored. I'd seen some of it and I was determined to uncover more.

I dish up Vivian's dinner and top up my wine glass. I was staying at Zach's tonight and he was driving, plus I still didn't have a car so I didn't need to worry about getting behind the wheel so another glass of wine wouldn't hurt.

Leaving Vivian with the TV and her food I head through to my bedroom to change for the evening, showering away the days grime before pulling on a pair of cut off denim shorts – tonight was especially humid with the promise of a storm – and an oversized jumper that hung off one shoulder. I kept my hair in the braid, letting it hang down one shoulder. I'd seen the way Zach was looking at it and I'm sure I'd soon find out if he liked it or not.

 I add a dress for tomorrow, my heels, a little number I hoped to wear for Zach, and toiletries plus underwear to an overnight bag and then carry it into the living room, dumping it by the door.

 "Going out?" Vivian asks around a mouthful of pasta.
 "Zach's."

 She wiggles her shoulders, "I hear wedding bells already."

 "Don't get too ahead of yourself," I laugh and glance at the clock. Harper still wasn't home so instead of texting, I hit the call button.

 "Hey," she mumbles, breathlessly.

 "You okay? It's getting late."

 She sighs heavily, "Yeah, the guys today really did a number."

 "What happened?"

 She huffs out a breath, "They hit a water pipe in the back and flooded the office so now I'm stuck trying to figure out what to keep and what needs to be reprinted."

 "Oh, Harp, I'm sorry."

 "I'm almost done anyway," She tells me, "Another couple of hours."

 "Did you need help?" I offer.

 "No!" Vivian all but screeches, "You're not forfeiting your night with Zach." She snatches the phone away from my ear, "Hey Harper, it's Vivi."

 Vivian nods and mm's and hmm's whilst Harper yammers on the other end of the line.

 "Okay, well I'll get a couple of people and we'll meet you down there."

Vivian listens and nods her head even though Harper can't see. "Sure, see you soon."

She hangs up the phone and passes it back to me, "Sorted."

"I can help," I tell her.

"No, what you need to do is leave with the man that is so clearly smitten with you and just enjoy a night for yourself. You do so much, you deserve it."

I sigh and pocket my phone, "But– "

"As your boss, I demand it."

I narrow my eyes just as the buzzer for the door sounds.

"Hello?" Vivian singsongs into the intercom.

"I'm here for Ray."

Zach's gruff voices settles deep into my core, the huskiness sending a chill that both warms and excites me all at the same time, tingling down my spine.

"She'll be right down."

Her finger releases the button and she cocks her head at me, "Go have some fun."

"Are you sure?"

"Never surer, you deserve this Raynie."

I pluck up my bag and pull her into a hug, "Thank you."

"Anytime," she says against my shoulder.

I head out into the hall and to the elevator. The butterflies in my belly really shouldn't be happening seeing as it's been a few days now and we'd seen each other naked but it's there anyway. I step out of the elevator and stop in my tracks, seeing Zach waiting just inside the doors for me.

His dark hair is pushed away from his face, his grey eyes sparkling with a subtle smile tugging on his mouth. He's dressed in a plain black t-shirt and dark jeans.

"Sweetheart," He breathes, "You ready?"

I gulp down some air and nod.

He grasps my hand in his and tugs me to where he's left his SUV idling on the sidewalk. You've got to have a lot of faith in humanity to leave the keys in the ignition running but then, as I walk up to the car I realise there's a driver sat behind the wheel.

I spin on the man attached to me by the hand, "What are you doing?"

"I wanted to share a bottle of champagne on the beach before dinner," he shrugs, "Is that okay?"

I nod, "More than okay."

He guides me to the back door and opens it for me, helping me inside with a hand on the small of my back. After he climbs in, he shuts the door and leans forward, murmuring something to the guy,

"You have someone else drive your SUV?" I ask.

"This isn't mine, WPS has an arsenal of these," he taps the black leather seat, "Julian up front is one of my guys doing me a favour."

"Oh wow," I smile, "That must be nice."

He nods once, "My guys, they're good."

"So you've been in this business long?"

"Mm," he nods, "Some time, but I don't want to talk about business."

He shifts closer to me as the car moves away from the sidewalk. If the driver is paying any attention, he doesn't show it. He's probably trained to ignore his passengers, it wouldn't surprise me if I could press a button and partition the front from the back.

"What do you want to talk about?" I ask.

"You."

"Me?"

He nods once, "Tell me everything there is to know

about Ray."

I laugh, "Not a lot. I like books, the beach and my friends."

"What about family, sweetheart?" He asks.

"My mom and dad are an hour down the road, only child and I once had a dog called Oreo."

His lips tilt up in amusement, "Is that all?"

"There's not much to tell."

"I don't believe that," he grins, "There's a lot to you, Ray, I don't care how long it takes me to learn it all just that I do, in fact, learn it all."

I blush, no one has ever been so invested in me before. The car pulls to a stop next to the beach and Zach climbs out, coming around to my side of the car to open the door for me.

As I'm standing on the sidewalk he goes to the trunk and grabs a small picnic basket and then grasps my hand, leading me to the moonlit sand. At the edge he stops to tug off his shoes, so I follow suit, stepping down into the fine powder and letting it seep through my toes.

We don't head too far, a couple hundred yards towards the surf before Zach stops, pulls out a folded blanket and lays it across the sand.

I sit, staring out into the darkened waves as he settles down besides me and pulls out two flutes and a bottle of champagne.

"Are we celebrating?" I ask, taking the offered drink.

"Mm," he agrees, pouring his own drink.

"What are we celebrating?"

He turns to me, the moonlight glinting of his silver iris's and holds his flute out to me, "Us."

Twenty-nine

Zach

"So, this was a household favourite," I tell Ray, dishing up the food, "We had it at least once a month which was never nearly enough."

She grins at me over the rim of her wine glass. Her cheeks are flushed, from the alcohol or the heavy petting I have no idea but it's a look I like on her.

I plate the asparagus onto the plate before adding the garlic infused chicken and buttered potatoes and then walk around to her, sliding it in front of her. She inhales.

"It smells amazing."

"Try it," I coax.

She spears a piece of asparagus onto her fork and takes a bite, closing her eyes as she chews.

"You really can cook," she muses.

"I wasn't lying sweetheart."

"I thought you might have said it to impress."

I laugh, "Do I need to impress?"

"Well I mean," she shrugs delicately, a smile teasing her lips, "You could ruffle those feathers a bit more. I'm not entirely convinced."

My eyes narrow in on her face, "You need convincing sweetheart?" I abandon the fork on my plate, grip her knees and spin her so her legs part and I'm inserted between them, "What part do you need to be sure about?"

Her blue eyes darken, "Well a number of things actually," she breathes. Her citrusy scent invades my senses and the way she looks at me from beneath hooded lids sends a shot of desire to my cock. I'd take her right now, I might just do that.

Her stomach grumbles. Loud. Her hand slaps across her mouth and colour pinks her cheeks.

"Eat, sweetheart," I command, "We've plenty of time."

Still blushing she turns back to her plate of food and digs in. The noises she makes, God, it's more erotic than any fantasy I've ever had and we're talking about food here. It's a struggle to get through the main course, my cock pressing heavily against the zipper of my jeans.

There's more to this relationship than sex, I need to show that but it's not far from my mind. I'm so attracted to the woman it's impossible to think about anything else.

After she polishes off the food I head to the fridge and pull out the cheesecake. Bought not made and cut two slices.

She's sipping on her wine as I slide it in front of her, her eyes glistening a tad from the alcohol.

"Are you drunk?" I question.

Ray snorts her laugh, "No, just a little warm."

"Warm, huh?" I slide a piece of cake between my teeth and pull it off.

"Mm, very warm," abandoning her cheesecake she climbs from the stool and steps away, "Mind if I get changed?"

"Go ahead, sweetheart," I gesture to the bedroom.

She smiles sweetly before picking up her bag and heading in the direction of the bedroom. I finish off the cheesecake and then take the plates into the kitchen, leaving them by the sink for the morning.

"Ray?" I call, picking up the remote for the TV, "Is there anything in particular you want to watch tonight?"

I try to think of the last time I had a woman in my home that I cooked for and then settled down for a movie with and realise *never*.

"I was thinking," the sound of her voice has me turning on the couch, my mouth dropping open at the sight of her, "We could find our own entertainment tonight."

I have no words. None.

Ray stands at the mouth of the hallway in nothing but a nude coloured body suit made of lace. It comes up high on her hips and low on her breasts and makes it look like she's wearing nothing at all. And whilst it is just an illusion it makes my blood pound as if she were spread out before me. Her glossy dark hair spills over both shoulders and one slender brow is arched.

Holy. Shit.

I scramble up from the sofa, my foot catching on the side table as I try to make my way hastily over to the beauty before me. I'm a mess of limbs and impatience, unable to quite find my footing which will close the gap between us.

Her eyes twinkle with amusement as she just stands there to watch me fumble.

I drop to my knees in front of her, my face burrowing into the soft patch below her naval, just above that heavenly place and groan, hands sliding up her bare thighs.

Her fingers slide into my hair and her laughter vibrates through her, "I assume you approve."

"You assume correct," I groan, pressing my mouth against her hip.

I'd never had a woman dress up – or down – for me.

I start to kiss down her bare hip, over the indent wear her thigh meets her abdomen and then further down over the tops her thighs, to her knees and shins whilst my hands skirt up the inside, the tips teasing the edge of the bodysuit that covers her from me.

Considering it's nude in colour, nothing is on show, much to my disappointment.

"I love this," I tell her, my voice more growl than anything else, "But it covers too much."

Her soft chuckle is like music to my ears.

I finally make it to my feet, cupping her face in my hands. I kiss her with a softness I didn't think possible in this current state of my mind but it's slow, languid, as my tongue penetrates her soft lips and the warmth of her seeps into my mouth.

"Do you have any idea what you do to me?" I ask against her lips.

She shakes her head subtly, never breaking the kiss.

"I wasn't lying when I said you make me crazy," I tell her, sliding my hands to beneath her ass and hauling her up, "So fucking crazy, All I can thinking about is you. Your kisses. Your body, your heat."

"Zach," she breathes.

"Tell me it's not just me," I growl against her lips,

"Tell me I'm not the only one."

"You're not," her hips grind, "I'm crazy too."

I hold her against me as I make the short distance to the bedroom, the movie forgotten. I lay her down on the bed, following her with my own body until I'm nestled between her thighs and staring down into the blue depths of her eyes.

"I'm going to make love to you tonight," I tell her in the pale light spilling in through the windows.

Her features soften whilst her lips part.

There was a difference between fucking and making love and with each flex of my hips into her, with each stroke of my hand and my tongue, every touch of my lips I made sure she knew the difference. I wanted to worship her. To light up her skin with feelings she wouldn't be able to compare to anyone else.

And when I made her come, I wanted it to be my name on her lips, never anyone else's. Her past can stay there, I want the now and the future.

Thirty

Ray

"Did you always want to be an assistant?" He asks into the dark of the room.

His hand strokes up and down my bare arm and his heartbeat is a steady thump in my ear where my head is pressed to his chest.

"No," I tell him, "I didn't really know what I wanted to do. I just sort of fell into it and before Vivian I hated it but now, I love my job. It pays well and I get to spend a lot of time with my friends. You can't ask for more than that really."

"I take it you've never had to deal with a stalker before?"

"No, this is the first time. I mean I've dealt with fan mail before, some of the stuff people send is crazy but it's never been threatening or violent."

He nods his head.

"What about you? Did you always want to go into security?"

"Mm," He grumbles, "I've never known anything else. It helps I enjoy my job. Same as my brother."

"Scott right?"

"Yeah."

"It sounds like you have a good support network."

"I do," he kisses the top of my head, "You must be exhausted."

I should be. I'm running on barely any sleep and only caffeine, but I also feel wired. Zach does that. He lights me up, recharges me, makes me feel like I could conquer the world. I glance at the clock on the bedside and see it's just after midnight.

"Are you?" I ask.

He tucks me in closer to his body, "Shattered."

I reach up and stroke my fingers down the side of his face, letting the tips tangle up in the hair scattered over his jaw. It doesn't take him long to fall asleep and whilst his muscles relax under me and his breathing comes in shallow even breaths, he never lets the arm curled around me fall away.

I tuck my face into his chest, inhaling his musky scent and close my eyes.

It didn't take me long at all to fall into a deep sleep which is why the sound of my phone squealing in the silence of the room startles me awake. I jump away from Zach's body, throwing myself out of the bed in a hurry to silence the thing so it doesn't wake him.

"Shut up, shut up, shut up!" I growl, fumbling in the dark for my clothes I had taken off earlier. My phone was still in the pocket. My hands finally land on it and I snatch it out of the pocket, turning the screen around to see Harper's name and face flashing across the screen. It's gone two in the morning, why an earth would she be calling for at this time!? Dread suddenly starts to weigh at my stomach, and I swipe the screen, answering the call.

"Two seconds," I whisper into the phone as I tip-toe to the door and gently pry it open to step out into the darkened hallway. I close the door behind me.

"Hey, sorry, I didn't want to wake Zach," I say into the phone, "Everything okay?"

A sniffle sounds down the phone.

"Harper?"

"Someone tried to break into the store," she sniffles, "I was still here and they smashed the front window." Her words come out in a rush, "I saw them by the counter and I didn't know what to do. They started to smash up the store but then Nate scared them off."

"Wait hold up," I shake my head, "Someone broke into your store?" Panic grips me, "Oh my God, Harper, did they hurt you?"

"No," she hiccups, "I'm okay."

"I'm on my way," I tell her, rushing back to the room to get dressed. I'm so focused on the call and keeping Harper on the line that I didn't see or hear Zach step from the room. I walk right into him, my head bouncing off his hard chest and then I stumble back, ready to land on my ass. His hands reach out quickly to grip me, holding me up from the tops of my arms.

"Hey," he soothes, "What's going on?" His thumbs smooth over my cheeks, coming away wet. When did I start crying? Why the fuck am I crying?

"Ray, you still there?" Harper asks quietly, her voice broken.

This has got to be *him*. He promised he'd hurt Vivian's friends. First it was me. Now Harper.

"Yeah," I choke out, "I'm still here. I'll be there soon,

okay? Are you on your own?"

"No," she shakes her head, "Nate's here."

"Nate?"

"Sandford."

Wait… "What?"

"Long story."

"Call the cops, Harp," Zach's still staring down at me, his brows pinched and mouth pressed into a thin line. I can't even enjoy his nakedness with the blood rushing in my ears and the dread weighing on my limbs.

"I already have, they're on the way."

"See you soon." I hang up and then stare at the phone. What the fuck was going on?

"Ray," Zach shakes me a little, "What's going on?"

"Harper's bookstore was broken into tonight," I whisper, "She was there."

"Okay," he nods, "Let's get dressed and go over, okay? It's going to be fine."

I nod, thankful that at least he's calm right now. I don't feel calm. I feel a war raging inside me. This has to stop.

He guides me into the bedroom and collects the clothes I wore over yesterday and then hands them to me before heading to his closet to dress himself. He pulls on a pair of grey sweats and a white t-shirt, watching me out the corner of his eye as if I'm about to break and shatter all over his floor.

Maybe I will.

I rub my arms, a chill settling over me. I didn't bring a coat. Zach strides over to me, dipping his head low to meet my eyes with a sweater clutched in his hand.

He tucks a finger under my chin and lifts my gaze from the floor, "It's going to be fine."

I nod, unconvinced.

"Sweetheart, I won't let anyone hurt you."

"It's not me," I breathe, "It's everyone else I worry about."

His eyes soften and he leans in, pressing his mouth to mine. "You're the kindest person I've ever met. Your friends are lucky to have you. "

He tugs his sweater over my head. The sleeves fall way past my hands and it's so big it falls way down my thighs, completely hiding my shorts under the deep burgundy material. The letters WPS are written in bright white across the chest. I curl my fingers inside the sleeves and tug my lip between my teeth.

Zach guides me to the door, plucking up the keys for his SUV on the way out. My legs carry me numbly down the stairs and out into the dark. I'm not even sure how I manage to get to the car but somehow I do and once inside Zach whacks the heating up and then reaches across, grasping my hand in his.

He squeezes my fingers, meeting my eyes for a moment as he navigates the roads of the city. His contact soothes me and eventually I squeeze his hand back, taking a deep breath in the hopes it'll stop my lungs from feeling so goddamn tight.

He never lets go of my hand, driving with one arm lazily hung over the wheel. His jaw is tight, the muscles pulsing as he grinds his molars and his eyes are like steel, hard and cold, staring out the windscreen.

The car rolls to a stop a couple hundred yards from the store. We're unable to get any closer due to the three cop cars parked out front and the ambulance.

I throw myself from the car. Why is there an ambulance? Harper said she wasn't hurt!

My legs carry me quickly over the sidewalk, the gap

between me and the store closing rapidly. Suddenly my waist is snagged by an arm banding around my middle and I fall back into a hard chest.

"Slow down, sweetheart, you don't want to go rushing in there. It's a crime scene."

I nod my head, understanding and take the offered hand Zach provides. My legs twitch to run but he's right, I can't just force myself in there.

"Behind the tape, ma'am," the uniformed officer stops our approach.

"I know the owner," I plead, "She asked me to come."

"Okay, she isn't inside," the officer advises, "She's over there with the paramedics."

Zach steers me away, "She said she was okay!" I cry, "She said she didn't get hurt!"

"Let's just go see her, okay," he soothes, wrapping me into his body. It should have been awkward to walk with me tucked under his arm like that but like everything else, Zach makes it effortless.

I spot Harper sitting on the sidewalk with a blanket over her shoulders and a bandage around her hand. Her hair is a mess and mascara tracks down her pale cheeks, her green eyes red rimmed and glistening. The blue lights from the vehicles flash off her face but she's not looking at me, she's looking at the ambulance with which the doors are still open. I can see two people moving around inside but can't see who they are working on.

"Harper," I call out. Her gaze snaps to me and fresh tears spring to her eyes. Her bottom lip drops and trembles and she starts to stand but then has to stop to steady herself. Zach lets me go to go to her, gripping her arm to help her back to the sidewalk.

"Ma'am," one of the paramedics chides, "Please stay seated, you've had quite the shock and you need to rest."

"You said," my voice breaks, "You said you weren't hurt."

She shakes her head and shrugs, "It's just a scratch."

With Zach on one side of her, I settle down on the other and wrap an arm over her shoulders, bringing her into me. Her shoulders shake with silent tears, so I hold her tighter, my eyes straying to the ambulance.

The paramedics part and the patient on the bed is finally visible. Nate. His face is a mask of frustration, his sandy coloured hair dishevelled, from the break in or his hand I'm unsure. There's a bruise forming along his jawline and his arm is wrapped from wrist to elbow in a bright white bandage.

"Seriously," Nate growls, "I'm fine. Let me check on Harper!"

"Mr Sandford," The same paramedic who chided Harper sighs, "We need to xray your jaw, you said he hit you with a crowbar."

"My jaw is fine," Nate growls, "If it weren't I wouldn't be talking now would I."

I had only met the guy a few times and we didn't really have much to do with each other, it was more Vivian but from what I could tell he was a nice guy. Nicer than you would expect him to be.

And he's just gone up a peg or two in my book, his genuine concern for Harper is palpable.

I want to question her on that but right now is not the time to do so.

When did they even meet?

"Sir, we can't force you, but we really advise a trip to the hospital."

"There you said it, you can't force me, now let me

up."

 I meet Zach's eyes over the top of Harper's head and all I see is amusement and…is that approval?

 What does Zach have to approve of?

Thirty-one

Zach

I couldn't blame this Nate kid, if my girl was sat on her own after something like this I'd be breaking down doors to get to her. Whilst it's stupid to reject medical attention after taking a crowbar to the face I can't judge him too harshly.

Ray's been staring back and forth for five minutes, clearly trying to piece together their relationship, her arched brows pinched in adorable confusion. At least she wasn't crying anymore. Shit, seeing that nearly split my chest in half. I never want to see her sad again.

Nate climbs from the back of the ambulance and starts towards us, stopping when he sees she's got company. His eyes narrow in on the space between my arm and Harper's and I grin, amused.

Oh this guy's got it bad. His good hand balls into a

fist and he stomps towards us. I could be a complete asshole right now and keep him guessing but I want my girl close. I push up off the ground, grinning at the musician. I pat his arm as I cross in front of him and then settle down next to Ray.

She doesn't realise she's doing it but her body curls into mine, even when she's still holding Harper.

The pure caveman look on Nate's face disappears as he realises who I am and then he sets himself in the spot I vacated.

"How you doing?" He asks Harper.

She nods her head, eyes snagging on the bruise on his jaw and wincing. She lifts her hand as if to touch it and then snatches it back, her cheeks flushing.

Ray's lips are pursed as she looks between them.

With Harper now settled a bit more I finally decide to start asking questions, "What happened, Harper? Go through it from start to finish."

Harper's green eyes widen on my face and her mouth opens and closes a few times before she sighs and sucks in a deep breath as if steadying herself to tell the story.

"Who are you?" Nate squares his shoulders as he looks over Harper's head.

Really, buddy?

"Nate, it's fine," Harper brushes her hand on his arm but he doesn't avert his eyes.

"Okay," Ray interrupts, pushing herself up so it disturbs the eye contact, "Look Nate, thanks for sticking around and all but you've probably got places to be."

"No, I'm good, Ray, thanks."

"Can I just talk now, please?" Harper snaps.

"Go ahead," I tell her.

"We had an issue with the renovations earlier, did Ray tell you?"

I shake my head.

"Anyway, we had a thing and I had to stick around to clean up a mess the builders left. Ray was going to come and help but Vivian offered instead, she bought a couple of friends, Nate being one of them."

"Vivian was here too?" I try to keep the frustration from my tone. What the fuck was that girl doing going out without an escort?

Harper nods.

"You knew about this?" I ask Ray.

She swallows and nods, "I'm sorry I forgot to mention it."

I squeeze my eyes closed and count to three.

"Go on," I grind out.

"Well they turned up and we managed to get it all tidied away. Vivian left about midnight with Oli, but Nate stuck around to help lock up. We were in the back, tidying a few of the boxes when we heard a window smash in the front. I went out to check and there," she visibly swallows, "There was a guy, he was dressed in all black with a mask on his face, it, uh, it covered half his face and then he started to smash up the store. He looked right at me."

Ray reaches out and touches her friends arm, nodding in encouragement.

"I didn't know what to do so I ran. Nate was just coming out the back when I ran into him, he confronted the guy."

My eyes bounce to Nate, "That how you got whacked?"

"Yeah," he grunts, "Fucker got in a cheap shot."

"Did you see his face?" I ask.

"No."

"They fought a little, Nate got hit and fell on the glass and then the guy ran, that's it. Do you think it's the same guy?"

Before I can answer, one of the officers walks over to us, purple shadows sit heavy under his eyes and his mouth is turned down in the corners, "Miss Lawson?"

"Yes?" Harper answers.

"Can we have a word?"

She nods and stands from the sidewalk, gripping the blanket around her shoulders as she follows the officer to the front of the smashed up store. I can't hear what is being said from this distance but whatever it is, it's screwing up Harper's face. She says something back but the officer simply shakes his head and her shoulders sag.

A few more tense minutes pass before she is striding back over to us, her brows drawn low.

"What did he say?" Ray asks.

"He doesn't think it's connected to the other case," she says, "he thinks it was just a kid trying to make a quick buck from the register."

"But there's no money onsite at the moment, it's been closed for weeks for renovations."

She sighs, "There's nothing they can do tonight, they're sending someone in to check for prints and stuff tomorrow."

"That's bullshit," I growl, "It's connected. The guy probably saw Vivian there earlier and wanted to scare her."

Ray winces.

"Wait, what are you talking about?" Nate asks, leaning over Harper.

"Doesn't matter. If there's nothing else to do, we should all just go home and sleep."

Harper nods and stands, Nate standing with her, "I'll take you," he says. I watch the two of them walk off towards a black BMW parked a little way down from the store. Ray scuffs her foot on the floor, the inside of her lip tucked between her teeth.

"You need to tell me when Vivian is planning to go out, what if she was there when he turned up?"

Ray drops her eyes to the floor, "If he knew she was there without security then he would have seen her leave."

My brows pull down.

"None of this makes sense," she presses a hand to her forehead, "Why wait until she leaves to smash up the place?"

"Well he's trying to scare her," I say but the words taste funny, *why* did he wait for her to leave?

Ray's phone buzzes in her pocket and she blanches, her hands shaking as she pulls it out.

"Who is it?"

She swallows but doesn't answer.

"Ray?"

Her eyes move over the screen and if at all possible, her skin becomes even paler, the colour draining from her cheeks, her lips. Slowly, she turns her hand around to show me the message.

I see you.

You look so good.

If only you could see me, sugar, you could see how good we are together.

It won't be much longer. We can be together soon.

I read it once. I read it again. There's no way he would be able to see Vivian in her apartment. It's got to be another scare tactic, but I call her anyway.

"Vivian," I say as way of greeting when she answers on the second ring.

"You're not Ray," she replies.

"You don't say," I deadpan, "Where are you?"

"Uh, at home?"

"Where exactly at home? Bedroom, living room?"

"Bedroom, Zach. Why?"

"Are you at your window? Are the lights on?"

"No, I'm in bed, you woke me up."

"Great. See you tomorrow."

"Zach – wait!"

I hang up the phone and hand it back to Ray. Her eyes are darting around, taking in the cops in front of the store, the paramedics packing up ready to head back to the hospital and all the dark spots in between.

Things are starting to click into place, that black spot becoming lighter. I make the decision to contact Scott in the morning, his eyes and his brain should be able to decode this. Fuck my pride.

I tuck Ray into my side, kissing the top of her head.

If my theory is correct, this woman won't be leaving my sight.

Thirty-two

Ray

I somehow manage to sleep, it wasn't restful and full of nightmares but I slept, even if I feel like death warmed up this morning.

"Why don't you stay here today?" Zach suggests over morning coffee.

"I can't just take a day off," I grumble, sipping at the scorching liquid.

"Why? I've already cleared it with Vivian. She can manage and I've got her schedule, I'm sure she'll survive without you for the next eight hours."

"Why did you do that?" I snap. "I didn't ask you to!" He cocks a brow at me and slowly lowers his coffee, placing it in front of him. I instantly feel guilty for the jab. I'm over tired. Over emotional and so damn confused it's hurting my brain.

"Sweetheart," Zach soothes, coming around the table

to crouch in front of me, he takes my hands from my lap and closes both of his around them, "It's be a chaotic few days. I know you didn't sleep well last night, all that fidgeting, I did it so you could rest."

I nod slowly. He was right. I needed a day. Just a day to get my head on straight. After that, I'm sure everything will just slot back into place rather than feeling like a really bad game of Tetris. I was never good at Tetris.

"Okay," I nod on a sigh, "Thank you."

"You'll stay here?"

"Sure," I nod.

He kisses my knuckles before knocking back the remaining dregs of his coffee and then disappears down the hall. I hear the shower turn on and not happy with the tension between us, I slip down the hall a few minutes behind him.

I can hear water splashing against the tiles and can see his muscled body moving, hands running through his hair. He's facing the wall, away from me.

I strip from my clothes, dropping them next to his and then pad naked over, opening the shower screen.

He startles and looks over his shoulder, his eyes darkening with every inch of my skin he takes in. The water is warm as I step under the spray and up against his back, my hands reaching around to press into his soapy abdomen. His muscles jump under my touch, his body going stiff as my nails dig into the flesh.

We don't say anything as he turns in my arms and leans down to press his mouth on mine. Water runs rivers over our skin, and as our kiss turns more passionate the air around us sizzles with anticipation. Surely it can't always be like this, so tightly wound, so charged there's a chance we're both going to explode and I'm not sure either one of us could survive.

His hands skirt down my body, his fingers digging in enough for me to feel the pressure but not enough for it to hurt and then he dips them between my legs, through my folds and hooks them, penetrating me.

I break the kiss, my head falling back as the pleasure of what he's doing ripples through my core. I'm shameless as I grind against his hand.

"That's so fucking sexy sweetheart," he growls against my skin, "Keep doing that."

I feel his eyes watching me but I can't stop, won't stop as he brings me ever closer to the edge of an abyss I don't mind jumping into.

He captures my mouth just as my orgasm begins to crest, swallowing down my cries and whilst I'm still pulsating, he spins me around and enters me in one swift movement. My hands land on the wall, my back bowing as I push my ass out and further into him. His hands land on my hips, fingers biting as he begins to pound into me, the water cascading over us only adding to the pleasure.

The quick succession of his hips brings a second orgasm roaring to the surface. My knees buckle but his hands hold me up and his thrusts do not relent.

"Zach!" I cry out, my fingers trying and failing to find leverage to cling onto.

He grunts and suddenly pulls out, his release spilling up my back.

I stay there for a moment, my arms leaning on the shower wall, my forehead pressed to the cool tile and then suddenly a sponge is swiped down my back, the scent of vanilla wafting passed my nose.

"Let me wash you," he says, voice husky and rough.

I nod and stand, turning so I can watch him work. His

eyes watch where his hands go and he's so gentle I can feel my heart swelling. He brushes the sudsy sponge around my breasts, down my stomach and then between my legs, his lips parting as he watches every movement of his hands. When he's finished, he gently tugs me beneath the spray, his hands chasing the bubbles from my body.

"I'm sorry," he murmurs against my hair.

"What? Why are you sorry?"

"I didn't – we didn't," he sighs, "I should have asked before we had sex to not use a condom. I just, I couldn't wait."

A small smile tugs on my mouth, Truthfully, I hadn't even thought about it.

"It's okay," I tell him, "I trust you."

He cups my face and kisses me, "I promise to always ask."

I grin, "Now don't go making promises you can't keep."

He chuckles against my mouth, "Okay, how about this?" He kisses the corner of my mouth, "I promise to never leave you wanting," his lips move to my cheek, "To always fight with you because *that* mouth," my jaw is next, "I promise to cook for you and bring you coffee. And I promise to protect you."

"Zach," I feel tears sting my eyes.

"Don't say anything, sweetheart."

So, I don't. Instead, I give it all back through my mouth. I give it back in the way my hands hold him close, in the way my eyes fall closed and my heart flutters in my chest.

After the shower we dry off and I pull on one of his t-shirts which only has him making grabby hands at me which I dance away from playfully. After that, I watch him tug on a pair of dark suit pants and a white button down, my mouth watering at the way the soft material falls over his sculpted body, a striking contrast to his tanned skin.

"Like what you see?" He teases.

I sit back on the mattress, propping myself up on my elbows, "Nah, I mean you could work on it a little."

He licks his teeth to hide his grin, "Is that so?"

I nod my head, eyes never straying far from the ladder of his abs.

"What am I going to do with you?" He finishes buttoning up his shirt and then strides over to me, kneeling between my parted thighs. The mattress dips under his weight and I drop down onto my back, staring up into his handsome face.

"I'm sure you could think of a few things."

"A few? More like thousands," his eyes twinkle as his hand whispers up my inner thigh, stopping just before the apex, "and once I've run out of those ideas, I'll just get creative."

"Go to work," I tell him, my voice far too soft and breathy, "I'll still be here when you get home."

"Good," he kisses me quickly and then stands, "There's a spare key by the door but let me know if you're going to go out."

"What? Are you my keeper now?"

"No," he smiles, "I'd just like to know so I know you're safe."

"Okay."

I see him out the door and then drop down onto the couch. It's really not safe to fall for him and yet no matter how many times I tell myself that I can't stop the feelings tightening my chest.

Thirty-three

Ray

It's been three hours.

Three hours since Zach left me on my own and Vivian agreed to giving me the day off. Three hours for me to lose my damn mind. I hate not doing anything. I hate lounging around the house whilst the world continues, and I hate having so much time to think.

If I think, my mind is consumed by images of mask wearing lunatics and violent messages and whilst I'm trying to push back the fear it's starting to ebb in at the edges.

I'd be stupid not to be afraid, even a little. Fear makes us human, it helps us survive, an instinct that keeps us from falling into harms way. Did I think this guy could do something to hurt me? Absolutely. Was I going to let it ruin me? Absolutely fucking not.

So, I get dressed. I pull on the dress I had packed for today and braid my hair and call Harper. Even if I'm not going to work today, I can still see my best friend.

"Hey Ray," she answers quickly.

"How are you today?" I ask.

"Good, I'm good, at the store now actually. They've given me the go ahead to clean up."

"Don't they have a team for that?" I ask, placing a few items laying out on the kitchen side back into my purse.

"They do, but I want to do it."

"Oh," I pause, "Okay. Do you want help?"

"Aren't you working?"

"Not today, apparently, and if I don't get of this damn house, I might go crazy."

"You're at Zach's?"

"I am."

"Sure, I could use some help."

"Great, I'll be there soon."

I order an uber and then text Zach, letting him know I'm heading to the store before bouncing down the stairs to wait for the cab.

The drive over is short and I can see Harper with a broom just inside the window, sweeping up the shattered glass from the hard wood floors. Before going in I grab us a couple of coffees from the café and then go in to meet her.

She smiles at me as I enter but I can't help the wince as I take in the damage.

It's not just the glass that's smashed, the guy took a crow bar to every surface within an arms reach meaning the counter, which had only just been replaced in the renovations had cracks through the wood, the shelves behind me had been pulled down but thankfully none of the books that usually lined these walls were out so they couldn't have been damaged in the break-in.

Harper's auburn hair is pulled into a high top-knot style but the usual shine in her emerald eyes has been dulled, diminished by the dark circles lining the underside of her eyes.

I hand her over the coffee and offer her a small, sympathetic smile.

"I'm so sorry this happened, Harp," I tell her.

She shrugs her shoulders, "It could have been worse. Vivian hasn't stopped calling, apologising like this is her fault."

I sigh, "Yeah, she did the same thing after the whole car thing."

Harper shakes his head, "This doesn't make sense, surely if you want to win over a girl, the last thing you should do is threaten her friends. How can he think this will win her heart?"

"The guy's sick, Harp," I sip my own coffee, "I don't think he understands his actions. He's got it in his head that they're destined for each other and will do anything to get his way. Even if that means destroying the people she loves."

"But he hasn't even asked her out or anything! She doesn't even know who he is!"

I shrug, "I don't claim to know the inner thoughts of this man, Harper, perhaps she's already met him, and she shrugged him off or told him no. We're not going to know until we find out who it is."

"Are you any closer to finding out?"

I shake my head, "The guys clever, he stays under the radar, I'm no cyber criminal but I guess what he's doing means the cops can't trace him."

"You'd think he would have gotten her personal

number by now," Harper says, resuming her sweep, "Rather than going via email, I mean if this guy knows so much about her, surely he realises you man her emails."

I pause. Staring at her.

That is a good point. I make a note to bring it up with Zach later but thinking about Zach, he hasn't texted me back. He's always been quick to reply and I know at this time, he'll be standing to the side whilst Vivian does yet another shoot downtown. I double check my phone to make sure I haven't missed a notification, but the screen is blank, save a few emails that's come in since I left the house.

I need to get a grip. I need to not think about work or the shitty situation we're all in and actually spend some time with my best friend.

"So," I continue, "Nate."

"What about him?"

"What do you mean, *what about him,*" I scoff, "You were with him all night! Nate Sandford! The famous musician!"

She shrugs, "He really doesn't come across as that guy. He's sweet."

"Sweet," I repeat.

"Yes, sweet, Ray, we're friends."

My eyebrows shoot up.

"What?" She snaps. "Can't I have male friends?"

I hold my hands up in surrender, "No you can, it just surprises me is all."

"You should get to know him, he's nothing like you'd think."

"I believe you," I say.

"Our friendship won't last though," Harper shrugs.

"Why not?"

"He's a big celebrity and I'm nobody."

"Harper," I scold, "You're amazing."

She laughs, "I'm fine with being nobody, you know me, I like to stay under the radar. Away from the spotlight. Being friends with Nate will drag me to places I really don't want to be."

I nod, understanding. Typical Harper. It's not a bad trait to have, her wanting to stay in the shadows. She sees everything there, listens without talking, and whilst she's come a long way since we were kids, she's still that shy girl that prefers to be neither seen nor heard.

Unless she's had a drink.

That's a whole different story.

"And you don't want to be friends with him?" I pry, "Or maybe a little more than friends?"

Her green eyes go wide, "*Noooo,*" She drags out the word. "That could never happen."

"Oh come on, Harper. I saw the way he was with you last night."

"What like you and Zach?" She wiggles her brows.

"Well I mean, if you're going to be like me and Zach then you're in trouble."

She blanches. "It's not like that."

"Does Nate know that?"

She shrugs, "I haven't given him any signals for him to believe otherwise."

"Mm-hmm," I purse my lips.

"Ray, seriously, it's *not* like that."

"Okay," I agree, "I believe you."

I so didn't believe her.

She narrows her eyes and then disappears out back to grab a dustpan and brush.

In the silence, my mind goes back to the fact that my phone has stayed silent since this morning. I didn't want to come across needy or desperate, but it worried me that I hadn't heard from Zach.

I tamper down the urge to text him again or call him and go about straightening out the store with Harper. She has some contractors coming out to board up the shattered window until the insurance will pay out for new ones to be installed so after we clean up, I head out to grab us some food and more coffee and then we spend the afternoon catching up.

It feels like it's been too long since we had some one on one time together when really, it's only been a few days, but I guess my life has gone by so quickly it just feels that way.

By four P.M. I feel much lighter. The stress that's been constricting my lungs has eased and whilst Zach still hasn't messaged me back, I don't feel like I'm walking a tight rope so much as a really rickety bridge.

I shovel a spoonful of icecream into my mouth and pick up the book Harper dug out from a box for me. There's a half-naked guy on the front, one with a billowing shirt and tightly corded muscles proudly displayed.

"Do all your books have these kinds of covers?" I grin. Not that I'm complaining. These books were always the best, the right amount of smut and romance to keep a girl going.

"No," she pouts.

"I was teasing," I wink, "You know I love them."

"Perhaps you should tell Zach to model for it," she teases right back.

My nostrils flare and she just grins.

"Evil," I shake my head at her, "Maybe you're not quiet because you're shy, maybe you're quiet because you're plotting."

"You'll never know."

Rolling my eyes I gather up my things, "I have to head off. It's getting late."

She nods, "Okay, will you be at home tonight?"

I shrug because really, I don't know. Zach's still not text me back, but I have to go back to his place to collect my things and he should be back by the time I get there.

"Just let me know," she tells me before pulling me into a tight hug and sending me on my way.

Whilst in the cab I try calling Zach. It rings a few times before going straight to voicemail.

Was he ignoring me?

If he was this was going to be really fucking awkward going back to his place.

Thirty-four

Zach

I collected Vivian and ferried her around the city to all her appointments and meetings. She was reserved today, her face a cloud of remorse.

By lunch time I'd had enough of her sombre mood.

"Vivi," I turn in my seat, looking to where's she's curled in on herself in the back. Her blue eyes meet mine, glistening slightly, "You want to talk about it?"

"What's there to talk about?" She shrugs, "My friends are being hurt because some psycho thinks he has some weird claim to me."

I wince, "Harper and Ray don't blame you."

"They should."

I look out to the huge skyscraper we were due to walk into in a few minutes and then back at the girl in the backseat. She looks so much younger when she's sad, so much more vulnerable than she'd ever let anyone believe.

That's one thing I'd learned in my time with these women, they were fierce. They were strong. And they were fucking loyal.

"I'm going to lay it on you now, Vivian," I brace myself, "Don't you dare let yourself believe that any of this is your fault. That guy, the one making your life hell right now? He's going to disappear and your friends, Harper, Ray, Oli, they are still going to be there. If the cops can't find this guy, *I* will. If not for you, then for selfish reasons."

Her brows pinch, "Selfish reasons?"

"He hurt *my* girl. In the process of hurting you, he hurt her and that, I'm not okay with."

"You really care about her, don't you? Ray, I mean."

"I do."

"Good. She deserves it but I will destroy you if you hurt her."

I chuckle, Hudson had threatened me and that was laughable, Vivian however, I believed that. I believed she'd castrate me if I hurt Ray. It wouldn't just be her either, the whole force would come down on me.

"I'm not going to hurt her," I say with conviction.

Vivian nods her head, "Good. That's good."

"Vivian," I try again, "Don't let this affect you. You're stronger than he is."

"I know," she sighs, "I just don't like seeing the people I love get hurt. Why can't he lash out on me? I'm the one he wants."

I shrug, "I can't answer that."

Her mood is only a little lighter when we walk into the building. I hardly pay attention to where I'm going, more to what is going on around me. I take in the suit lounging nearby, a phone by his ear and the vendor a few feet away selling takeaway coffee and hotdogs. I watch every man and woman walk by us, trying to figure this shit out.

Despite the conversation with Vivian, I was really starting to suspect this had nothing to do with her at all.

I walk her to the floor in which her shoot was taking place, see her through the doors and pull out my phone, settling down on a couch close by. I call Scott.

"Zach," he beams, "God, I've had more calls this week than I've had all year, what's going on?"

"You know the job I'm on? And how I sent off that sample?"

"Yeah?"

"I might need your help."

"I'm sorry, what?"

I roll my eyes, "I don't have time for jokes, Scott. I need your help with this. A fresh pair of eyes. I'm missing something and I can't figure it out."

"I'm not joking around, bro, tell me what you need."

I explain it all. The emails, the threats and the vandalism on both Harper and Ray.

"And this Ray? She's your girl?"

I clear my throat, "Uh, yeah."

"Case aside, are you serious, Zach, you go get a serious girlfriend and you don't tell me?"

"We're not kids, Scott," I play it off, pretending I don't hear the hurt in his tone, "I didn't realise I had to give a daily update on my love life."

Truth be told we told each other everything, all through our teenage years and into adulthood. I was the first to know he had gotten his short-term girlfriend at the time pregnant and she wanted to abort. I was the one he confided in when he begged her to keep the kid and give it to him when it – she was born which eventually she agreed to. I was there the day my niece was bought home from the hospital. We did it all together. Keeping this – Ray from him was a low blow on my part.

He clears his throat, "Can you send me everything on email?" He asks.

"Sure, I'll send it after the call."

"Is that everything? There's nothing missing?"

"Not that I can think of."

"And there's no one you've met in the past few weeks that could be your suspect?"

I think about everything that's happened, my mind snagging on one thought, "There was a guy at the club. He seemed shady to me."

"Okay. Then it's not him."

"What?" I sputter.

"It's too obvious."

I roll my eyes, "I don't really think that's how this works."

"Of course, it's how it works. You're thinking about this too logically, take a step back, detach yourself from the situation and really look."

"I'll try," I grumble. I thought I had been doing that, "I'll send over the material now. Let me know if you get anything."

After I hang up, I collect everything Ray's received via email and send it across to my brother. Giving him a bullet pointed list of other things that have happened, including the car. At the same time, I submit the paperwork I had been neglecting to submit, the ones which includes me pounding in that guys face.

After I'm done, I place the phone down on the couch besides me and run my hands over my face.

God this was such a fucked-up situation.

I'm still cradling my head in my hands when the sofa dips besides me.

"Mr Wyatt," a familiar male voice says besides me. My muscles bunch up and my blood pounds furiously as I crack one eye open and look to my left.

Rage blows up inside my veins and my vision blurs as I look at the man to my left.

"You've got about two fucking seconds before I throw you through the nearest wall," my voice comes out deadly calm despite the war inside my body.

"Perhaps you could let me explain."

"Explain what?" I growl at him, "How you enjoy scaring women and touching them without their consent? How about the fact that you bruised *my* girlfriend?"

His eyes narrow, "Your girlfriend?"

"Yeah buddy, *mine*," I didn't care how possessive I sounded. Ray was fucking mine. Not his. Not anyone's. *Mine.*

"It's not like she told me she was taken." He says, his voice snarky.

"It's not like she said yes either." I bite back.

"I was just coming over here to tell you I wasn't going to press charges, you know for the incident back at the club."

I smile. It's not a nice smile. "Well good for you. I can't say the same for Ray though. I have advised her to seek legal help for the way you handled her back in the club."

That was a lie. Amazingly, I delivered it without my usual tells.

Sam licks his lips, "Fair enough."

"Fair enough?" I question.

"Is she here? I'd like to apologise."

"No," I growl. "And you're never going to go near her again, you hear me?"

"Loud and clear," he smirks.

"Is that why you're here?" I ask, pushing down the bloody images from my head. The ones which show me what it would be like to smash his face in with my fists. "To find Ray?"

"I work here," He shrugs like it's no big deal, leaning back into the couch and kicking up one leg to rest his ankle on his knee. "My studio, it's below this floor. I saw you walking up."

"Then you would have seen Ray wasn't with me."

He smirks again, "You're right. I knew she wasn't with you. But not because I didn't see her."

"What the fuck is that supposed to mean?"

He shrugs, "I'm glad she's happy with you." He says but his tone suggests otherwise, "I guess she'll never know what it's like to be with a real man."

A bark of harsh laughter leaves my lips, "You've got to be fucking with me."

"Hardly. You're just a glorified guard dog. One that bites none the less. They should really put you down."

I squeeze my eyes closed. This fucking guy. As if I didn't have enough on my plate, now I had to fight the urge not to kill a man and go to fucking prison.

"I suggest you go climb into your hole," I snap at him, "Before I bury you in it."

"Sure, man," he slaps a hand against my upper arm, "See you around."

He stands from the couch and tucks his hands into his pockets, grinning down at me.

"I'm going to start counting," I tell him calmly, "If I get to five and you're still there I shan't be held accountable for my actions."

He chuckles lightly and then strides away.

I count to three and when that doesn't work, I move to ten and when that still doesn't work, I snap up from the couch and storm down the stairs and out the building. My fist connects with the nearest wall, the knuckles splitting immediately. Blood spurts from the open wounds and my skin begins to bruise but I don't feel the pain. My anger, my frustration it masks and numbs it all.

It's taking everything in me not to climb those stairs, find the guy and *destroy* him.

I pace the sidewalk for at least twenty minutes, my breaths coming out in short, sharp bursts hoping my heart doesn't pound out of my chest from the way it is slamming against my ribcage.

This type of anger, it was ferocious, dangerous even, as in, if I were really stuck in the same room as him, I honestly think I would kill him.

The thought really should snap me back to reality but my vision, it sees red.

I need her. I need Ray.

Thoughts of her start to push the impulses down. Her voice. That's what I need.

I dig my hand into my pocket, looking for my phone but come up empty. Slapping my hands over every pocket I realise I must have left it on the couch upstairs because every pocket is empty.

There were still too many hours left in the day, too many hours to count down before I could get back to her and settle the fire burning in my soul.

Thirty-five

Zach

"What's gotten into you?" Vivian asks, sitting up front with me rather than in the back.

I grunt my response.

I didn't find my phone and because I didn't have it, I couldn't tell if Scott had found anything, both put my mind deep in the gutter. Chances are someone snagged my phone after I raged from the building earlier. I had found a first aid kit to seal up the cuts on my knuckles but as for the anger inside me, yeah there was nothing much to quell that.

"Zach, what is it?" Vivian demands as I pull up to her apartment building and kill the engine.

"Nothing," I snap, going around to her side of the car to help her out. She's already climbing out by the time I get there, her eyes glowering at me.

"Don't be a dick, Zach."

"Can you make it from here?" I snap.

"I'm not a child, I won't get lost on the way to my own apartment."

"Good."

I watch her stomp into the building and to the elevator. She waves stiffly to the concierge before climbing into the metal cart. The doors close behind her, and I wait a few more minutes to make sure she gets inside okay.

I then throw myself into the driver's seat and barrel it home.

My mind focused on one thing and one thing only.

Ray.

I have no idea if she's tried to contact me.

My parking is atrocious, more abandoned than anything else and then I'm taking the stairs two at a time, my legs closing the gap between me and her quickly. My body and mind are working in unison. The one goal clear. The door swings open after I unlock it, my chest heaving like a madman and then I see her. Curled up on the couch sleeping.

Her knees are locked into her chest, her dark glossy hair falling down over her peaceful face whilst her lips are parted and her lashes flutter against the apples of her cheeks.

I swallow hard before closing the gap.

Dropping to my knees I press my face into her stomach, inhaling her scent deep and tangling my hands around her ankles gently.

It's an instant balm. A cool water that settles over my skin and stills the raging blood in my veins.

I have no idea how long I stay there. Ten minutes, twenty, an hour…who knows.

Something touches my head, fingertips pressing into my scalp as delicate hands run through the strands.

My head snaps up and I meet her blue eyes, still slightly hooded with sleep. A small smile tugs on her mouth. "Hi," she rasps.

"Baby," I groan, dragging her onto the floor with me. She comes willingly, falling into my lap and allowing me to wrap her in my arms to hold her tight against my chest.

"Hey," she soothes, "What's the matter?"

I shake my head against her body, not willing to relive it.

"I need you," I beg.

"I'm here," her voice wavers and when I meet her eyes, her brows are pulled down in concern. "Did something happen with Vivian?"

I shake my head and press my mouth to hers, allowing her lips to further extinguish the burn inside me only for it to ignite another.

She whimpers under me, her arms coming around to hook my face to hers. She shifts her little body until she is straddling my lap and grinds herself into my painfully hard cock.

"It appears you missed me," she muses.

I don't answer, I just show her. I show her how much I missed her, how much I *need* her. With my hands and my mouth and my body.

We end up in bed, her naked and tangled like a vine around my body and finally I can breathe. I can see and think clearly.

"Are you okay?" She asks, concern etched in her tone.

"I am now," I admit, running my fingers down her spine.

She's still naked and sprawling across me, her sweet breasts pressing into my chest. She looks so much better than this morning, rested and rejuvenated.

"I'm sorry if you text me today," I tell her, "I lost my phone."

"Lost?" She questions, "You didn't lose it. It was here the whole time."

"What?" I jump up so quickly she practically falls off my body but I'm quick to hold her to me, moving her so she sits by my legs.

"I found it when I got back from being with Harper. It was on the coffee table when I got back."

My brows pull down. That's not possible.

I *had* my phone. I called Scott from it.

"Where is it?" I ask.

"Still on the table."

I throw the sheets off and bound from the room, finding my cell exactly where she said it would be. On the coffee table, face down. I unlock it and check my calls. I definitely called Scott, it was right there in my call log. Plus, I had a few missed calls from Ray and a message to tell me she was heading out.

I stride back into the room. "When did you get home?" I demand.

She shrugs, "After five maybe? I thought you would be already be here."

"Vivian's meetings ran late," I grumble, "And you're sure this was here when you got back?"

"Yes, Zach."

This didn't make any fucking sense. How the hell did my phone end up back here after I had it?

"What the hell is going on?" Ray tucks the sheet around her naked body, her brows pulled down in concern.

I just shake my head, "I need to make some calls this evening."

"Do you want me to go home?"

My head snaps back, "*No.* Why would I want you to go home?"

"What happened to your hands today, Zach?"

Like a child, I tuck the injured hand behind my back, trying to hide it from her. "Trapped it in a door."

"You're lying."

I should just tell her I ran into that dick of a guy today, that he got me so angry I punched a fucking wall, but then the thoughts swirling through my head might start swirling through hers and I don't want her to worry.

"Please stay," I change the subject, "order take out and we can watch a movie or cuddle or something, just don't go."

Her body softens and she smiles up at me, those pretty eyes glistening. My chest tightens as I look down at her, the mere sight of her there, on my bed, calming the storm threatening to rage inside me.

When I've sorted this shit out, when I have the answers I need, I'm going to really need to look at the feelings she's stirring up inside. It's not like anything I've ever felt before.

Before I head through to the office I lean down and gently press my mouth to hers, feeling the soft pillowy lips part ever so slightly as her tongue brushes against my bottom lip.

I dress and I leave before I join her on that bed and head to the office, clicking the door closed behind me as I settle into the leather chair behind the desk.

I open my emails and search for something from Scott but when nothing is waiting for me in the inbox, I dial my brother.

He picks up almost immediately but doesn't speak. I hear my little niece giggling in the background, her innocent laughter filling my ears.

"Shh, shh," Scott chuckles, "Your uncle is on the phone."

"Uncle Zach!" Her tinkling voice yells, "Uncle Zach, let me speak to him!"

There's a shuffling sound and then her cute little voice trickles through the speaker, "Hi uncle Zach."

"Hi Fee," I say, "You keeping daddy on his toes?"

"Just like you taught me," she confirms proudly.

"That's my girl!"

"Daddy said you have a girlfriend."

"Did he now?"

"Hey give me that," Scott brings the phone to his ear, "She's a gossip."

"Mm-hmm," I laugh, "I was actually calling wondering if you had a chance to look at the stuff I sent over."

"Shit sorry man," he sighs, "Between that paperwork you sent over and a few fires at the office I haven't had a chance to really get into it."

I nod even though he can't see, my hand scrubbing across my jaw.

He fills my silence, "What the fuck are you doing fighting in clubs anyway!?"

"He deserved it. Did you read the full report?"

"Yes, Zach, I read it all."

"Okay, I don't need a lecture. I need help. Can you try get round to looking at it soon?"

"I'll get on it tomorrow, okay?"

"Okay," I sigh.

When he hangs up, I sit in the silence of my office until the noise of the TV starts to trickle beneath the door and the mouth-watering smell of food makes my stomach growl.

When I come out of the office, I find her in the

kitchen, cooking, dressed in only that oversized sweater I let her wear the other night. Her long tanned legs dance around the kitchen whilst a movie plays in the background.

I come up behind her, not realising she's got a pair of earphones pressed into her ears. As my hands grip her waist, she jumps so high and then spins, whacking me straight across the face with the spatula in her hand. Well shit.

Thirty-six

Ray

"Zach!?" I screech, ripping the buds from my ears. "Oh my god! I'm so sorry!" His eyes are squeezed shut, his face scrunched up as a bruise begins to form across his left cheekbone.

I dash to the freezer and grab a bag of frozen peas, wrapping them in a towel to press to his face.

"What the hell were you thinking, sneaking up on me like that!?" I whisper hiss, pressing the peas to his face.

"I didn't realise you were listening to music," he says gruffly, wincing as I move the peas to sit better over the bruise.

I've been a bit jumpier as of late anyway, I suppose that's normal with everything going on but shit, I hit him!

"Least I know you can defend yourself," he huffs out

a laugh.

"Hardly," I scoff, "I had a weapon."

"A spoon."

"A spatula actually." I wave it in front of his face.

"I'm so sorry, let me get a look."

I move the peas away, lightly pressing my fingers to the welt, "Does it hurt?"

"Like I just got hit with a spoon."

"Spatula," I huff, shaking my head.

I'm still inspecting the forming bruise when his arms snake around my waist and he drags me into him, "I know how you can make it up to me."

"God, you're insatiable," I laugh into his chest even though his words sends a fire through my veins, turns out I'm insatiable too but I need food first.

"Only with you." To prove his point, he presses his growing erection into me.

"I just hit you and you're getting hard, there's something wrong with you. I think you need help."

He barks a laugh, "You're probably right."

"Anyway, I need to cook before this burns," I wiggle from his arms, "Reckon you can resist your urges for an hour?"

"Well I mean, if I *have* to I will but I'm not going to like it."

I roll my eyes, "You're so dramatic."

He settles onto a stool, pressing the peas to his face whilst he watches me continue to finish up dinner.

"I want you to learn self-defence," Zach says as I stir the mushroom sauce.

"What?" I frown, "I can defend myself."

"Oh yeah?" I turn at his incredulous tone, seeing his face twisted in disbelief.

"I can!" I defend.

"Okay, well after dinner you can show me what you can do and if I think it needs work, we're going to do lessons."

"Why do I need to learn self-defence?"

His silence has me turning again, "Zach?"

"I just think everyone needs to know it."

"So, you're going to teach Vivian and the others too?"

"No. Just you."

I roll my eyes.

"What? I'd rather you know how to defend yourself."

"Do you think I'm going to need to?"

He shrugs and swallows, "You never know."

I take in the sudden tension in his shoulders and what looks like pain in his face, "Does your face hurt?" I ask.

He shakes his head.

He's been acting strange since he came in this evening. Stiff, shut off. Pushing away my curiosity I finish off the food and begin to plate it up, sliding one in front of Zach and my own in the spot next to him.

We eat in silence, the sound of the TV behind us the only noise to join the clink of forks on china.

—

"Show me," Zach orders, setting his legs shoulder width apart.

I tug at the hem of the sweater, "Zach, is this really necessary?"

"Yes, show me sweetheart. Show me what you're made of."

I stare at him, taking in his wide shoulders which tapers down to his chest and waist, the muscles on his abdomen which right now, look formidable. He's huge. I mean I knew what I could deal with in a

240

situation and he wasn't it. He could crush me with his hands!

"Zach," I plead.

"I mean, if you don't think you can do it."

My eyes narrow, "Excuse me."

Just because *I* was thinking it doesn't mean I want other people thinking it too.

"I suppose we can get you some pepper spray, do you have a gun license?"

"I don't like guns."

He snorts. "You don't have to like them, you just need to know how to use one."

"Do you have a gun?"

He nods his head once.

My mouth forms a little O. It shouldn't surprise me really.

"Have you ever used it?"

"At the range," he shrugs.

"So you've never shot anyone?"

"No, Ray, I've never shot someone."

I tug my bottom lip into my mouth.

"You have two options, sweetheart, learn how to defend yourself or carry protection. Choice is yours. I'd actually prefer you had both."

"Why are you saying all this now?"

His shoulders stiffen, "It's important. Now show me, Ray."

"What do you want me to do?"

"Take me down."

I eye him again, taking in his size and height. How the freaking hell am I supposed to take *him* down

"Zach, you're so much bigger than me."

"You think you'll always be fairly matched in a fight?"

"Well no, but I'm also not planning on getting in any fights."

"You never know, Ray, now take me down."

Swallowing, I charge at him. I've watched the videos, there's certain things you can do to take down an opponent and yet when I hook my leg around his and use my elbow to force a hit into his stomach he barely even moves. Not even a grunt.

Suddenly I'm spun, my back to his chest with his arm wrapped around my chest, holding me in place.

"Is that all you've got, sweetheart?" His voice is in my ear, a whisper. "Get me off."

I squirm which only makes that arm around my chest tighten. When that doesn't work, I simply try tugging on it which of course does nothing.

"Zach," I whine, "I can't do this. I'll just scream."

"And what if you're somewhere private?"

"I really think this is unnecessary."

"We'll train an hour a day," he lets me go, "It's late now anyway."

"What aren't you telling me?" I ask.

"Let's go to bed," he deflects, pressing a kiss to my hair before trudging down the hall and disappearing into his bedroom.

I stand for a few minutes and then follow after him, climbing into the bed and curling into his side. He drags me closer so there's no air between our bodies and that's where I fall asleep, safely cocooned into this warrior of a man.

Thirty-seven

Ray

I sit up front with Zach when we drive over to Vivian's the following morning. He's quiet, a permanent crease on his brows. The bruise from the hit last night is more of a shadow than anything else this morning.

"Zach," I repeat for what feels like the hundredth time and he finally flicks his eyes to me.

"Sorry, did you say something?"

"Don't worry," I turn to watch the city rolling by the windows.

"Okay."

Zach waits in the car as I head into Vivian's apartment, waving to Thomas as I climb into the elevator and head up. I unlock the door, finding Vivi in the kitchen, that blender whirling a bright pink liquid today.

She smiles but it barely reaches her eyes. "Hey, how you feeling?"

I nod, "Rested. Thank you for letting me have yesterday."

"You do too much," she waves a hand, "You deserved it."

Why was everyone acting so strange? First Zach, and now Vivian.

My phone buzzes in my pocket and I jump. Fuck. This guy was in my head!

When I pull out my phone, I see it's just an email from Hudson and shake my head. I was going to go crazy by the time we manage to stop this creep. And the cops, ugh, they had nothing either!

"We've got the second half of that shoot this morning," I tell Vivi, "And then a meeting with the marketing team at that cosmetic company you did a commercial with last year. Looks like they're looking for a new face for their brand."

Vivian nods, "I liked them."

We walk back down the car together, finding Zach leaning like he always does on the side of the car, those dark glasses wrapped around his eyes. He smiles tightly at Vivian and opens the back door, his fingers brushing down my spine as I climb in after her.

The silence in the car is so thick you could cut it with a knife.

I didn't like this at all.

Zach pulls the SUV into the parking lot behind the huge office building, his entire demeanour shifting to something almost feral. His eyes blaze whilst his jaw clamps so tight it's got to be painful for his teeth. He's not even looking at us as we climb from the back of the car, his eyes are on the building. What the hell is going on?

Nerves bubble through me.

I need to get it out of him. He walks behind us as we head through the large glass doors and straight for the elevator.

We climb into the cart but before the doors can close, a hand darts out to stop them from shutting and then a face I'd hoped to never see again steps in.

His eyes are lit up but it's not friendly.

Zach curls a possessive hand around my shoulder, subtly pulling me back until I'm pressed up to his chest.

"Oh my God, Sam?" Vivian smiles at the photographer, "It's been a while!"

I sigh. She has no idea *who* he really is, what he's really like and now is not the time to get into it.

"Vivian," He smiles at her, "How nice to see you. Ray." He greets me, eyes lingering on the hand on my shoulder.

If anything, it only makes Zach tighten that grip. I don't step away from him. This guy, he doesn't make me feel safe at all. Vivian continues to chat with him but the entire time he looks at me, his mouth set in a grim line, eyes narrowed.

The doors finally open on our floor and Zach practically drags me from the cart, tugging Vivian along with us.

"Did you not remember him?" Vivian asks as we head down to the studio.

"No, I did." I nod.

Zach's walking incredibly close to me, his arm on mine.

"Oh, you didn't speak to him much."

"Sam's…" I trail off trying to think of a way to explain it.

"An asshole." Zach finishes. "One you'd be wise to avoid."

"Oh," Vivian gasps, "Why?"

"Just stay away from him," Zach warns, "Reckon you can do that?"

Even I wince at his tone, "Hey," I grab his arm, pulling him to a stop, "What the hell is going on with you?"

"Nothing," he grumbles.

I look at the time, "I need to get Vivian inside, but this isn't over, you're going to tell me whatever it is that's got you like this."

He stares down at me and for a minute I think he's going to tell me to fuck off but then a heavy exhale comes from his mouth and his eyes soften, "Okay."

I nod, "Okay."

We walk into the studio with Vivian, doing all the necessary things to get her ready for the remainder of the shoot and once she's safely in front of the camera, I drag Zach over to the corner of the room, far enough away so people can't hear us but close enough that I can still see Vivian. Zach's staring down at the couch a few feet away, confusion tugging at his brows.

"Spill it. What is up with you?"

"My phone yesterday," he starts, "I had it. Here. I was on the phone with my brother on that very couch before it went missing."

"Zach," I shake my head, "You sure you're not confused, it was right there when I got home, what you think someone found it and broke into your place just to return it?" I laugh, how ridiculous, right?

Only Zach isn't laughing. Not even a little.

"Shit, you think that happened!?"

"I had my phone, Ray," he pulls it out of his pocket and brings up his call list, showing me a call he made earlier on that day. I feel the blood drain from my face.

"I think there's more to this than we originally thought," he scrubs a hand over his face, "I think we're looking at it wrong. I've got my brother working on it too."

"Do you have any idea?" I press, my heart thumping in my chest.

He shrugs his shoulders and looks away. He knows or at least thinks something, but he doesn't want to share.

"Zach, whatever it is, you can tell me," I say softly, touching his arm, "I can handle it."

When he meets my eyes again he looks…tortured. Like whatever it is he thinks this to be physically pains him.

"Just please," He tugs me into him, "Please *stay safe*."

"You're scaring me now," I tell him.

"Let me figure it out okay, let me think about this." I nod, unconvinced.

Zach's in and out for the rest of the day, making calls and each time he returns, that stony expression just settles further onto his face.

By the time we're leaving the meeting that afternoon, I'm physically exhausted.

Hudson offers us all to dinner, having met with us for the meeting this afternoon and whilst Vivian accepts his offer, I shake my head.

"I was actually going to head home, but enjoy guys." Zach's torn between me and his duty to stick with Vivian.

"It's okay," I tell him softly, "I'm just going to head home. I'll see you tomorrow."

"Ray," he steps away from the others for a minute,

gently tugging me towards the car, "Come to dinner. Stay with me."

I shake my head, "I'm tired, Zach, I just want to stay at home tonight."

He searches my eyes, "Please."

I kiss him, "I'll see you tomorrow."

I step away and hail a cab.

I feel his eyes on me the entire time, my skin feverish, my muscles tight. I meet his eyes from the window of the cab and then I'm pulling away, disappearing into the thick traffic of downtown.

My bed, my own clothes and a nice hot bath is all I need right now. I just need some space to think.

I pay the driver and head into my apartment building, the familiar blue carpet and beige walls of the foyer settling some of the unease inside me.

Yeah, this is just what I need.

Thirty-eight

Zach

I don't eat with Hudson and Vivian, I stand off to the side watching the restaurant move around me. Seeing but not really taking in. Scott still hasn't called me back. At all. I've called him at least ten times today and each time the call has gone to voicemail or not gone through at all. He said he'd get back to me today but it's now way past six and all I've had is silence.

I tug a hand through my hair, feeling my frustration right down to my toes.

Next to me Vivian laughs at something Hudson said but all I can think about is Ray. Did she get home okay? Is she tucked up on her couch right now with Harper watching a movie and eating popcorn? More importantly, is she safe? She text to let me know she was home but I haven't heard from her since.

Finally, the two of them wrap up their meal and I follow them out onto the sidewalk. The sun has started to dip in the sky, night pressing in and whilst the sky is clear and the air warm, I feel a storm brewing.

"Have a good evening," Hudson pats me on the back and then leans in to kiss Vivian on the cheek, lingering a little too long for it to be friendly and then he's walking in the opposite direction, back to his car. I guide Vivian to the SUV and take her home, showing her in and to the elevator.

I'm just climbing back into the SUV, Ray's contact information up and ready for me to hit dial when a text comes in.

I read the words, my blood running cold whilst my heart picks up speed.

No.

No. No. No.

Scott: You need to get back to Seattle. Tonight. Dad's not doing so good. He's in the hospital.

No!

I hit the call button at the top of the message, but it just rings out.

I smash my hands against the steering wheel. Not now!

I can't deal with this right now!

I throw my phone onto the passenger seat and wheelspin out into the road, heading in the opposite direction to Ray's.

This can't be happening. I pick up my phone again and dial my brother but he still doesn't pick up, so I call Ray. She picks up on the third ring.

"Hey," she breathes, "I was just thinking about you."

"Ray," my voice cracks. I can't lose my dad. Not yet.

"Zach? What's happened?"

"It's uh, it's my dad. He's in the hospital. I need to

get back to Seattle."

"Okay, okay," she soothes, "Are you on your way to the airport?"

"Yeah," I grunt, "I'm going to get one of the guys to fill in for me for a few days whilst I'm gone, okay? I'm not going to leave you alone."

"Don't think about me right now, Zach. I'm fine. You just get to your family okay?"

"Ray?"

"Yeah?"

"You are my family too."

She sucks in a breath, "Zach, why did you say that?"

"I don't know." I admit. "I just know I need you, sweetheart."

"I need you too." She breathes.

I nod my head, "Okay. That's good."

She laughs, "It's going to be okay."

It wasn't going to be okay but I don't say that out loud.

"I'll call you soon," I promise.

"Just do what you need to do, Zach, don't worry about me."

I scoff and then clear my throat. I'll always worry about her. Especially right now.

"Bye sweetheart."

"Bye Zach."

She hangs up.

I hit dial on the office number and wait for someone to answer, when they do, I demand I'm put through to one of my head guys. I won't leave the girls stranded. I order for one of the best to be there in the morning and then try Scott again. No answer.

What the fuck was he doing!?

And why the hell did he text me to tell me about dad?

That was not like Scott at all. He called. Always.

I pull into the airport and park the car. I haven't even packed any shit and I have no idea how long I'll be in Seattle.

Thankfully, I'm able to get flight tickets but the flight isn't for another three hours so I head to a coffee shop, my stomach a ball of knotted nerves.

Something wasn't quite sitting right.

I try Scott's phone. *Again.*

When that fails, I text him back.

Update me. What's going on?

As I sit there, the smell of coffee sticking up my nose, I re-read the message he sent.

It's not so much the words that are making me question *everything*, it's the fact that there are no messages before this one. That can't be right. I've text Scott from this phone before, hell before I got so busy with Ray and the girls we text near enough everyday to check in so where the hell are all the messages?

I never delete anything. It's a weakness on my part, a hoarder if you will. Don't even get me started on my email account. Nothing gets deleted, just archived.

I click through the settings on my phone, just to make sure I haven't changed anything but when it's all as it should be I go back to my texting app, leaving it on the home page so it shows all the messages I've sent and received.

Scott first, then Ray and then…Scott again.

That's not right.

I take a sip of my scorching coffee and then take a deep breath. Maybe I'm just overtired, overworked, and so freaking confused I'm seeing things incorrectly.

Squeezing my hands until my nails bite into the palms and shaking my head I try again, reopening the app and looking.

It's the same.

Oh no.

Oh *shit!*

Instead of hitting call from recently dialled I scroll my contact list and find two Scott's. I only know one.

I double check the numbers and dial the one not tried today.

As I'm staring down, my brow puckered the thing starts to ring in my hand. I hit the button as quickly as I can, holding the phone to my ear whilst the blood rushes to my ears.

"Scott?"

"Hey, Zach," he sounds tired, "Sorry I haven't called."

"Is dad okay!?" I hiss into the phone.

Silence.

"Scott! What the fuck happened? Why is dad in the hospital?"

"Dad's in the hospital? I just saw him."

Dread settles into my stomach and I stand abruptly from my chair, knocking it back. It clatters loudly against the floor and I ignore the heads that turn my way.

"What do you mean you just saw him?" My legs eat up the space between me and the exit, "You text me. You told me he was in the hospital."

"Uh, no, Zach. I didn't."

I knew it. I fucking knew it. And I ignored my instincts.

"Shit!" I bark.

"Zach, what the fuck is going on?"

"Did you look at the shit I sent you?"

He sighs heavily, "Yeah, I did."

"And?" I press, slamming my way through the doors.
"Have you maybe thought the guy isn't after Vivian?
After looking at your reports, plus the emails, it looks
more like the guy is trying to get Raynie Stone's
attention, rather than Vivian's."
I suspected as much.
Shit.
"Scott," my breathing is coming out too quick, I can
feel my lungs constricting. "He's after my girl."
"You knew, didn't you?" Scott asks.
"I didn't know," My legs feel like jelly as I finally
make it to the SUV and I practically fall against it, "I
suspected."
"I can't confirm," Scott says, "Only assume."
"Did you get a new number?" I blurt.
"No, man, same number as always."
It hits me. Like a freight train.
Someone – *he* – wanted me away tonight. He wanted
me away from Ray.
He fucking planned it. And was successful.
"Fuck!" I bark.
"Zach, what the–"
I hang up the phone, rage bursting through my veins.
No one will touch my girl.
Once I'm in the car and on the road, I try calling her.
No answer.
I try again and again and again.
No answer.
What if I'm too late?

Thirty-nine

Ray

When I got home, Harper was just heading out, her auburn hair pulled into a low hanging ponytail which she had draped over one side. She looked cute in a pair of tight blue jeans and a white blouse.

To my complete surprise, Nate was here too.

"Hi Nate," I said, curious, "What are you doing here?"

I'm almost immune to celebrities now. I've met so many that their stardom, their fame, and their glory, it really didn't do anything for me. I could appreciate the man was handsome, very much so, but he was still just a guy. One who happened to hit the big bucks with his voice.

"Hi Ray," he smiled warmly as Harper joined him by

his side.

There's something going on there. I had pressed her for more information, but she insisted they were just friends and were going out for drinks this evening. I was invited along but I really just wanted to have a bath and put my pyjamas on and then watch a round of really crappy TV.

The phone call with Zach had tightened the band around my chest. I felt for him. I really did. It's got to be hard being so far away from your family all the time, especially now that his dad is sick.

Hearing that panic in his voice, the shake to his usually confident and firm tone, it damn near broke me.

I cared deeply for Zach. More than I probably should this early on, but it was him.

I always knew he'd rob me blind, I always knew he had the potential to steal my heart and not give it back and yet I took that risk.

It was worth it.

"You are my family." He spoke with such earnest, with such conviction, I believed it.

I really hope he is okay. I really hope his dad pulls through.

The sadness I feel for him, it has me dialling my own dad. We spoke for about twenty minutes, just digressing everything going on in our lives and at the end of the call I told him I loved him and then hung up.

I've been vegging on the couch ever since, a pair of low hanging cotton pants covering my legs and the sweater I stole from Zach. It still smells like him.

It's been a few hours since I spoke to him on the phone, but I don't call or text, he could be on a plane back to Seattle by now anyway.

I switch the TV off and stretch out.

It's been so hectic over the past few days, it's been hard to breathe and it feels like forever since I've been home.

Zach's place is beautiful, the view of downtown extraordinary, but nothing quite beats the sound of the waves crashing on the shoreline. I step out onto the small balcony I have with my shared apartment and breathe in the salt tinged air.

There's something calming about water.

It's been too long since I actually got to swim in the sea. Too long since I lounged on the beach with a book, my toes buried in white sand, the sun on my face.

I listen to the waves for a while, a harmonic hum that fills my ears and eases my soul. I'll always be a water girl, no matter where I go, or who I go with, it's what I will always seek.

After a while I realise I've left my phone inside and panic, what if Zach tried to call with news? I should bring it out here.

And whilst I'm at it, I can get a nice glass of wine and can enjoy the peace for a while.

I step back into the house and head to where I left the phone on the coffee table. I press the button to light up the screen, seeing I've had several missed calls.

Three from Zach. Two from Harper.

I'm just about to call Zach back when an email comes through.

Knock, knock.

It's from him.

What the hell?

Knock, knock.

The sound of knuckles on wood echoes in my ears.

I just stare at the door.

Knock, knock.

The raps seem to pulse through my body as my heart leaps into my throat.

Keeping my phone locked in my hand I tip-toe to the door and gently press my face to the peep hole.

Sam's face comes into view.

My phone buzzes.

I can hear you. Open up.

Oh!

I stumble back from the door.

A loud thump sounds, and then another. It doesn't take me long to realise it's him throwing himself against the wood separating us.

Holy fuck. What do I do?

Thump.

Thump.

I run.

The apartment isn't very big though and there isn't many hiding spots. In the closet. Under the bed. All the spots he'll find me.

Whilst he continues to batter at the door, I dial the police.

"Uh" I huff, slipping into Harpers' bedroom and shutting the door with a quiet click, "Someone's trying to break into my apartment."

I go through the details with them, my hysteria building with each thump that reaches my ears. A sudden bangs has a squeak escaping me and I drop my phone.

When I pick it up the line has gone dead.

It's okay, I breathe.

They've already dispatched someone.

Help is coming.

Without really thinking, I hit the call button next to

Zach's name.

"Ray," he answers immediately, "Where are you?"

"He's here," I cry, trying to muffle the sounds of my sobs.

"Who?"

"Sam."

Silence.

"I think it's him. I think he's the one who's been stalking Vivian, but I don't think it's her he's after," I whisper.

"I know."

I don't have time to process.

"What do I do?"

"Baby," Zach's voice has a soothing edge, but I don't miss the panic, "Can you hide?"

Panic claws at my throat, my air coming out too quick and too shallow, "Nowhere. To. Hide." I pant.

"A weapon, Ray, get something to protect yourself with," he's trying to stay calm, I hear the effort, but I also hear the fear in his own voice.

Another large bangs resounds through the apartment, the same sound a door makes bouncing off a wall.

"Ray!" Sam's voice bellows through apartment.

"Zach," I squeak.

"I'm coming!" Zach barks, "I'm fucking coming, Ray."

"Where are you, sugar?" Sam asks.

I hear his footsteps against the hardwood floors, getting closer and closer to the door. I press my hand over my mouth.

"I know you're here, don't you know I know everything about you, Ray?"

I scoot further into the room, ducking down beside Harper's bed on the side furthest from the door.

Zach's breathing sounds through the speaker on the phone.

"I know it all." Sam continues, "Did you not know it was me?"

Harper's door swings open and light floods in. I duck down, I know he's going to find me and yet I can't bring myself to move.

"There you are," Sam's voice is soft but it doesn't match his hard face or the wild look in his eye. "Why are you hiding from me, Ray?"

A whimper leaves my mouth.

"Ray?" Zach asks on the phone.

"If you leave now," I breathe, my voice shaking, "We can forget this. I'll tell the police it was all a mistake."

"A mistake?" Sam crouches by my feet, his hand reaching out to touch a slither of skin on show at my ankle, "Why would it be a mistake?"

"Why are you doing this?"

He cocks his head to the side, "We belong together, Ray."

My head snaps back, so hard the back of my skull bounces off Harper's bedside table.

"Ray, get out of the apartment," Zach begs. He had been talking but I didn't hear anything he was saying. "Get out. Hit him and run. I'm almost there."

Where the hell was the police?

"Sam, I think," I stutter, "I think you need to get some help. We – we don't belong together."

His face twists and he grabs my ankle, wrapping his fingers around and tugging me down. I slide towards him, almost dropping my phone in the process.

"We do!" He bellows, "Life gave me a second chance," he tells me, "You look just like her."

Nausea rolls through my stomach, bile pushing up my throat.

"Look like who?"

If I keep him talking then I give myself time.

"Ray, just get out," Zach bellows down the phone. The sound of his voice has Sam's eyes flicking to the device.

"Who are you talking to, Ray?"

Menacing. It's the only way I can describe him right now as his eyes darken and his mouth twists.

"No one," I lie, taking the phone away, "No one at all."

"You wouldn't be lying now would you, Ray?"

I shake my head.

"Hand it over."

"Please," I beg.

"Give it to me!"

A strangled sob leaves my throat as I hand over the phone, Zach's name still illuminated on the screen.

He looks down at it and then lifts the phone to his ear, "Hello, Mr Wyatt, she won't be needing you anymore. Don't come here and don't go near Ray ever again."

He clicks the phone off and turns his attention back to me.

"I'm disappointed, Ray," he sighs, "You've disappointed me, do you know what that means?"

I swallow.

"It means you need to be punished."

Forty

Ray

"Get your hands off me!" I scream as he drags me by my ankle back to the living room. I kick and I try to grasp things as I pass them, but I can't get a good grip on anything. My palms sweat and my heart thumps wildly.

Survive. I need to fight. I kick the heel of my foot into his palm, hitting my own ankle in the process but the pain doesn't quite register.

"Stop fighting, Ray. I gave you options. I gave you me and you declined."

"What!?" I screech, "You forced yourself on me!"

I grab the leg of the table, forcing it away from the wall with a screech. Sam tugs hard, dislodging my hand but as it does the table tips, the contents on top spilling off the edge. A large hardback book smacks me on my left eyebrow. Stars burst behind my eyes.

"Now look at what you did," Sam tuts.

Numbness floods down my limbs but he's let me go so I try to get away, pushing my lethargic body up onto my elbows and trying to shimmy my body away.

It does no good. Sam steps over my body and grabs my arms, pulling me to my feet. My knees buckle, my head spinning.

Who the fuck knew books could be so damn dangerous!

I feel a warm trickle of liquid running down from my eyebrow.

Snap out of it, I order myself, shaking my head to try and clear the fog. Sam hauls me over to the couch and drops me unceremoniously onto the pillows. As he turns to bring the coffee table closer I notice the gun tucked into the back of his black jeans.

Swallowing hard, I press a hand to my forehead.

"Sam, you don't have to do this," I slur.

"Oh honey," Sam sits, "I do."

"Why?"

"Because," he shrugs, "My wife. She was taken from me. It's not fair. And then I saw you and you look just like her. It's a sign. We belong together. We've always belonged together. A second chance."

"I'm not your wife," I tell him.

"No," he shakes his head, "But you'll do."

"You need help," I spit, "You're fucking crazy!"

A palm hits the side of my face.

Anger bursts through me, pushing away the dizziness, "How dare you!" I kick out my leg, hitting him square in the chest, causing him to topple back. I use it to dart up from the sofa, heading for the front door which whilst closed has holes in the panels from where he forced himself in. My hand wraps around the handle. I can taste it. Freedom. Safety.

A hand twists in my hair and I'm tugged back, my neck snaps back painfully.

"Help!" I scream, strangled, "Someone help me!"

There's no other apartments on our floor but there are above and below us. The floors are thick but if I'm loud enough, maybe, just maybe one of the other residents will hear me.

My body is tossed down onto the floor, his hand still tangled in my hair as he straddles my hips and sneers down at me. He must twist his hand more as the sting from my hair being pulled tingles across my scalp and I have to grit my teeth.

"My wife was a little rebellious too," He growls, "I put her in her place."

"You sick fuck!" I spit.

He reaches out to run a finger down my face using the hand not gripping my hair. I snatch myself away, my breathing rough and violent. He grips my chin tightly, forcing my face back to his. He bites his fingers in, forcing the soft tissue on my cheeks to press into my teeth. The metallic taste of blood flows over my tongue but I don't show him he's hurting me.

"Zach's going to kill you," I goad, "He'll be here any minute and he's going to rip you apart!"

He lifts my head and slams it back down. It ricochets off the hard floor and I wince, pushing the darkness edging in away, clinging onto my precious consciousness. Just a little bit longer.

"Don't ever mention him again!" Sam barks, "Never again"

I grin, the best I can. It's probably slightly manic.

"What are you going to do, Sam? You lost your wife, you're not going to hurt me."

His anger is palpable.

"Don't test me, Ray," he sneers.

Behind his back I see a flicker of movement. A flash of red.

"You and me," I spit, fidgeting under him, "we'll never be together."

He raises his hand as if to hit me but then a loud crack echoes into the room and his body falls to the side, freeing me from his weight.

Forty-one

Zach

My tyres screech as I slam on the brakes outside of the apartment building. Behind me I see flashing blue lights, the wail of sirens but I'm not waiting for them.

She needs me.

My girl needs me.

The car has barely stopped by the time I'm throwing myself out the door, leaving it wide open, keys in the ignition, as I slam myself through the front doors of the building and up the stairs. I have no time to wait for the elevator. I take the stairs two at a time, getting to her floor quickly.

My heart pounds fiercely in my chest, the blood rushing in my ears. Her door comes into view, wide open and the sound of crying fills my ears.

"Ray!" I yell, pressing harder on my legs to close the

gap between us. I cross the threshold but stop dead in my tracks.

Ray and Harper sit huddled on the floor, a discarded baseball bat by their feet whilst Sam lays unconscious next to the couch.

Holy shit.

Ray's crying, Harper's sobbing.

Shaking out of it I cross to the girls, pulling Ray from Harper. She comes willingly, falling against my chest as fresh sobs break from her throat.

"Baby," I breathe, touching over her body, "I'm so sorry. I'm so fucking sorry!"

My eyes flick over to Sam, he's still breathing and then I look to Harper who's shaking.

"Did you hit him?" I ask.

She nods slowly.

"Well done, Harper. You saved her."

You saved her when I couldn't.

Chaos ensues a few minutes later as a swarm of uniformed officers burst into the room, guns drawn.

"Get on the floor!" One of them yells, "Let her go and get on the floor."

Gently, I place Ray down on the couch and step back, holding my hands up, "It isn't me you're after."

"Get on the fucking floor!" He yells.

"Officer!" Ray begs, "It's not him. It's him," she points to Sam's stirring body. "He attacked me."

The officer looks to the floor and then gestures for his team to surround the guy just coming to.

He lowers the gun pointed at my chest and nods once.

—

Ray steps out of the cubicle they had been hiding her in ever since we got to the hospital a few hours ago.

She's still in the clothes from earlier, a low hanging pair of pyjama pants and my sweater. Her brow has been stitched up but that looks like the worst of her injuries, thank god. Her eyes are red rimmed, dark purple shadows sitting just beneath and her mouth is set in a grim line.

I stand the moment I see her coming, crossing the space between us, and dragging her into me. She falls against my chest, her hands resting on my pecs as she breathes in deep.

I smooth a hand down the back of her head, snapping my hand back when she winces.

"It's okay," she says before I can apologise.

"I was fucking terrified," I whisper to hide the shake in my voice. "I've never been so scared."

"Your dad?" She questions.

I shake my head, "It was fake, he sent the message to get me away. The police confirmed earlier they found the message on his phone."

"Wow, he went to a lot of trouble."

I nod grimly, "He's a troubled man."

She huffs out a laugh without humour, "You can say that."

"Let's go home," I wrap an arm around her. She freezes, stiffening in my arms. "My home," I clarify. "Harper is staying with Vivian."

She relaxes and lets me guide her from the hospital, out into the growing light of early morning. I help her in the SUV and then climb in the other side, taking a deep breath.

I glance over to her, watching the way she curls in on herself, bringing her knees to her chest and wrapping her arms around them. My hands tighten on the steering wheel. I startle when a hand lands on my forearm.

When I look over, Ray is staring at me, a softness in her eyes I've never seen before. "Let's go."

I nod jerkily, turn the key, and pull on to the empty street.

When I park the SUV and climb out, Ray wraps her hand in mine, sighing deeply.

I could have lost her.

I could have lost something that hasn't really started. The feeling inside my chest, the sheer terror I felt at knowing she was hurting, and I couldn't be there, fuck, I never want to feel that again. I never want to be without her again.

I pull her to me, holding her tight as I bury my face into her hair. Emotion builds at the back of my throat, stinging my eyes and I just inhale. I have no idea how long we stand there, in the growing light of day, her wrapped in my arms where she'll never leave again. I don't care what I have to do to keep her there. I don't care what I have to sacrifice, I'm keeping her.

Eventually we head inside and straight to the bedroom where I curl my body around hers, holding her to my chest as exhaustion claims her.

"I'm so fucking in love with you," I whisper into her neck, "it hurts."

She starts to fidget, first turning onto her back and then onto her side, facing me. Her eyes are open, hooded with tiredness but she's very much awake. A small smile tugs at her mouth, "I love you too."

Forty-two

Zach

It's been a few days since the incident with Sam. A few days for life to settle back into some resemblance of normalcy and a few days for Ray to become a little more relaxed. She cries out in her sleep a lot, lashes out in her dreams but it's getting easier, though there's a long road ahead of her.

Sam was obsessed.

His apartment was covered in images of Ray, in every aspect of her life, from grocery shopping to the night I caught him with Ray in the club. There were images of Ray next to his wife and the resemblance was really quite startling, though there's no relation there.

The police found several computers in his house, hundreds of email accounts, and equipment to hide him from being found out. He had always planned this. Getting to Ray using the email address for Vivian because she was always on it. He'll be sentenced in a few weeks.

The apartment has been fixed, a brand-new door installed with locks – installed by me – that'll take a god damn tank to get through. I won't risk her safety. Never again. Even though she's been staying here since then.

We go to bed together, wake up together and eat together.

I'm still going to work with them everyday but eventually they won't need me anymore. Yes, Vivian is popular but it's nothing she can't handle herself and we'll be available for her during the big events.

Ray saunters over to me, the little red bikini she's wearing barely covering her body and my mouth waters, eyes taking in her smooth skin and toned muscle. She curls into my lap, instantly causing all the blood in my body to head south. She wanted to swim today and I wanted to watch.

Water drips down her skin and she leans in, pressing her mouth into mine, "What are you thinking?"

"That you're never wearing this bikini out of this building."

She laughs, a sweet, tinkling sound, "Is that an order, Mr Wyatt?"

"Mm," I grunt, "The only person who gets to see you like this, is me, is that understood?"

She smiles, her eyes lit up, "As much as I dig the whole alpha thing you got going on, I'm going to have to refuse."

I narrow my eyes.

"But what I will promise," she presses her round breasts against my chest, the material slipping dangerously low, "is that only *you* can see me without any clothes on."

I reach around and squeeze her ass, "That's a given."

"Presumptuous," she shakes her head, "Do you know what assuming does?"

"All I'm hearing is ass," I tell her, "And how fine this one is."

She chuckles lightly, "You're an ass."

"I'm wounded," I mock offence.

She pouts playfully," Terribly sorry, how can I make it up to you?"

"Kiss me," I growl.

Her smile turns mischievous as she presses a delicate kiss to the side of my lips. My mouth chases her as she retreats. My fingers bite into her ass and my teeth grind.

"That's not what I meant."

"Isn't it?" She asks innocently, "Then show me what you meant."

I grab her hips and force her to straddle my lap, pushing my hard cock up into her delicate flesh and eliciting a delicious moan from her. As her lips part and her eyes darken with desire, I slam my mouth on hers, abusing her mouth with my tongue. Her hips move shamelessly and if I don't get a grip now, I'm going to pull her panties to the side and slide deep inside her, privacy be damned.

"Get your ass upstairs," I whisper harshly in her ear, "Now Ray before I do something that'll get us both in trouble."

Her eyes widen slightly and when she climbs from my lap, I miss her heat immediately. We hurry to the elevator that'll take us back to my condo and when the metal doors slide closed I press her into the wall, dipping my hips to brush my cock against her clit through the thin material of her bikini.

Her breathing becomes rough and her fingers claw at my shoulders.

I'm still holding her as I walk out of the elevator and to my front door. I practically fall through it trying to get in so quickly.

We're too lost in each other that I don't see the person waiting just inside the door.

A throat clears and my spine stiffens.

My mouth breaks away from Ray and I find my brother standing there, arms crossed over his chest, one of his dark brows cocked.

"Fuck!" I bark, dropping Ray and shoving her half naked body behind my back.

"What the fuck, Scott!?" I bark.

He grins, amused, eyes darting to Ray who's peering around my arm.

"Eyes here," I demand, "Not on her."

This just makes him smile harder, "A little possessive, little bro."

"He's *very* possessive," Ray tuts, stepping out from behind me to extend her hand to my brother. I growl as his hand envelopes hers, only seeing the fact that she is half fucking naked in front of another man.

Fair to him however, his eyes never stray from her face.

Ever the gentleman, my brother.

"I'm Ray," she smiles, looking at me from over her shoulder. A curled strand of hair brushes against her bare shoulder.

"Scott, you must be the girlfriend I've heard so much about."

"I guess I am," she says. "I'll leave you two to it, I need to put some clothes on before he bursts a blood vessel."

Scott bursts out laughing, "Good idea."

I watch Ray saunter away, her hips swinging, round ass swaying and suck my tongue back into my mouth. Scott never looked once. When she's safely tucked behind my bedroom door I turn my attention back to my brother.

"What are you doing here?"

"I came to see you, Zach. It's been a shitty couple of weeks and after what happened, I needed to make sure my little brother was okay."

I sigh and then step forward, hugging my brother, "I'm good man."

"Looks like it," he laughs, "She's pretty."

"Don't," I grunt in warning.

"What I can't even tell you your girl is pretty? Wow, I never thought I'd see the day my brother fell in love."

I roll my eyes, heading to the kitchen to get a bottle of water. I toss one to him and unscrew the cap on mine, taking a healthy swig, hoping the ice cold water is going to cool me down. Ray does shit to me, she turns my blood molten and I need relief.

"You look good," Scott says after a beat, "I trust LA life suits you."

"I'm good, now that this shit is over, I'm good."

He nods, "Good."

Ray chooses this moment to come out of the room, dressed in a flowing cobalt blue summer dress with her dark hair pulled across one shoulder.

"Where are you going?" My eyes rake down the front of her, taking in her luscious curves and long tanned legs.

"Out with the girls," she grins, "You're both coming."

Forty-three

Ray

Zach holds my hand tightly, his shoulders stiff. I don't blame him. The last time we were in this club, Sam was here but it's over now and it's time to move on.

I drag Zach through the heaving crowd towards the VIP area, his brother, Scott following behind. The bouncer waves us through and I spot the girls, along with Hudson, Nate, and West in one of the booths at the back. Scott's only visiting for a few days but it's nice to see Zach with his family.

My heart literally sings when I'm with him. It's crazy to believe how we started ended up to where we are now, but I wonder if because of that, it's the reason I fell so freaking quickly.

"Ray!" Vivian jumps up, holding a flute of champagne, already swaying in her sky-high heels.

Hudson reaches out and grips her waist, steadying her form before snatching his arm away and knocking back the amber liquid in his glass. When we reach the table a glass is shoved into my hand and I slide into the booth next to Harper.

She smiles at me, looking so much better than she did a few days ago when I last saw her. Apparently seeing your best friend being attacked by someone and then saving them really takes it out of a girl. Who knew?

Nate is close to her side, they're not touching but the way he looks at her, he's smitten. She claims they're just friends though.

Oli is batting West's wondering hands away, chastising him but she clearly loves it if the gleam in her eyes is anything to go by.

West meets Zach's hand and then he's introducing Scott to the group.

As I sit there, sipping at the bubbles in my glass I realise how fucking good I have it.

Sure, a load of shit happened but I have such a great team behind me, even the guys are part of this. It started out as just the four of us, us girls against the world and somehow, we built *this*. A family.

Tears sting my eyes and gratitude fills my chest.

"Hey," Zach whispers, his brows pulled down in concern, "Are you okay? Do we need to leave?"

He's been walking on eggshells around me for the past few days, I didn't blame him but I was ready to start moving forward. Sam's gone. I don't have to worry about him anymore and whilst I have no idea how long it'll take, I know I'm okay.

"Fine," I lean into him, feathering my fingers down his face. His eyes fall closed and he leans into my touch, his breath fanning across my palm. "Just happy."

"Me too, sweetheart." He murmurs, pressing a kiss into my palm.

After a few more drinks, I stand from the table and head to the dance floor, Vivian on my heels. I knew she'd be up for a dance.

We dance and laugh to the music, her hand in mine and it isn't long before the rest join us, save for Scott and Hudson who are still at the table, watching us all. They're talking but it doesn't seem like an in depth conversation, especially not with the way Hudson's eyes burn into Vivian's flowing body. She dances sensually even when she doesn't mean to.

Zach slips up behind me, wrapping his arms around my waist. I lean into him, feeling all of his hardness. He trails kisses down my ear and over my jaw, fingers spread across my lower belly. We dance like that, not even in time to the music, but more to our own beat.

"I love you," He whispers in my ear, "I'm still not used to saying it, I don't think I ever want to stop."

That makes me smile, "Then don't."

"Marry me."

I stop moving. "What?"

"Marry me, Ray," He spins me in his arms, his grey eyes looking down into my face, "Marry me. Right now."

I laugh and press a kiss to his lips, "How about, yes, I'll marry you but let's actually plan it?"

His brows crease but then his eyes light up, "You said yes."

"I did."

"You want to marry me?"

"I do."

"Holy shit."

I roll my eyes and kiss him. It turns hot really fucking

quick and he presses his growing erection into my lower belly. "Home. Now." He demands.

We don't say goodbye, he tugs me through the club and into a waiting cab, only letting go of me to help me into the seat. When I'm there, he pulls me into his side and kisses me hard.

"Extra tip to get us there in ten," he tells the driver.

When we pull up to the house seven minutes later, he throws a hundred onto the passenger seat, lifts me from the cab and carries me into the building.

"Put me down, caveman," I giggle.

"Never."

And he's true to his word, carrying me all the way to the condo, through the door and down the hall into the bedroom before he gently lays me down on the bed and slowly undresses me. With the way he looks at me I already feel naked, it's so raw, so hot, I have no idea how I'm ever going to get used to his intensity. He removes his own clothes before climbing up between my legs and rubbing the head of him against my core. His mouth steals my moans, his hands claim my body and when I'm a writhing mess beneath him, then, and only then does he sheath himself with a condom and slide in deep.

He fucks with abandon, alternating between rough, deep thrusts and slow, sensual pulses, his hands seemingly everywhere.

My body reaches a peak and when I'm falling, my body spasming around his, he declares his love for me over and over again, his own release chasing mine.

We lay in bed, my head on his chest, the only sound coming from our breathing.

I had no qualms about living my life like this. With him. And only ever him.

"Tomorrow," I say into the darkness, "Let's get

married tomorrow."
 He pulls me up and crushes his mouth to mine,
"Tomorrow."

Epilogue

Zach

I had never been so sure of anything in my entire life. Sure it was quick, no one knew that more than I did but knowing that Ray would be mine forever pushed any worries from my mind.

She walks towards me in a knee length white gown with sleeves that sit off her shoulders. Her dark, glossy hair is down, cascading over her back and her make up is light. Vivian, Harper, and Oli walk behind her in matching dresses but in different colours. My brother slaps a hand against my arm.

We couldn't get married immediately, much to my dismay but managed to plan something for just a few short weeks after my proposal.

I was actually glad for that, my brother came here, along with my dad and my niece. Ray's parents were also here and the smile I saw on her face when they arrived a few days ago was enough to make the wait worth it.

She meets my eyes as I stand at the end of the aisle and beams at me, the blue of her eyes electric.

I don't wait. As soon as she's in arms reach, I grab her and pull her to me, slamming my mouth on hers, pretty lipstick be damned. The crowd chuckles and I know I really need to let her go but God she feels good.

"Bro," Scott clears his throat, "You might wanna save that for *after* the ceremony."

I grin at my soon to be wife, noticing how her lids are hooded and her eyes have darkened.

I can't wait to get back to the hotel room. I can't wait to strip her from this dress and taste her on my tongue.

Something settles in my soul when I slip that ring onto her finger and we're declared husband and wife.

I scoop her up and kiss her again, my tongue sweeping inside her mouth.

"Mrs Wyatt," I taste it on my tongue, "Mine."

"Always." She declares.

ABOUT THE AUTHOR

Victoria McFarlane is an indie author new to the Contemporary Romance scene!
In between writing, she's a mother and a wife and if she hasn't got her nose in her laptop you'll find her reading.
She lives in the south of the UK, close to both the coast and the beautiful New Forest.

Avid lover of gin, cowboys and bad dad jokes!

Want to keep up to date?

Head on over to social media to catch up on exclusive sneak peeks, upcoming releases and all things books!

Instagram: victoriamcfarlaneauthor

Facebook: Victoria McFarlane Author

Made in the USA
Middletown, DE
11 March 2022

62512756R00172